About Jessica Hart

Jessica Hart was born in West Africa, and has suffered from itchy feet ever since, travelling and working around the world in a wide variety of interesting but very lowly jobs—all of which have provided inspiration on which to draw when it comes to the settings and plots of her stories. Now she lives a rather more settled existence in York, where she has been able to pursue her interest in history—although she still yearns sometimes for wider horizons.

If you'd like to know more about Jessica, visit her website: **www.jessicahart.co.uk**

Hitched!

Jessica Hart

First published in Great Britain 2012
by Mills & Boon, an imprint of Harlequin (UK) Limited.
Harlequin (UK) Limited, Eton House, 18-24 Paradise Road,
Richmond, Surrey TW9 1SR

© Jessica Hart 2012

ISBN: 978 0 263 22833 5

Harlequin (UK) policy is to use papers that are natural, renewable
and recyclable products and made from wood grown in sustainable
forests. The logging and manufacturing process conform to the
legal environmental regulations of the country of origin.

Printed and bound in Great Britain
by CPI Antony Rowe, Chippenham, Wiltshire

Also by Jessica Hart

We'll Always Have Paris
The Secret Princess
Ordinary Girl in a Tiara
Juggling Briefcase & Baby
Oh-So-Sensible Secretary
Under the Boss's Mistletoe
Honeymoon with the Boss
Cinderella's Wedding Wish
Last-Minute Proposal

Did you know these are also available as eBooks?
Visit www.millsandboon.co.uk

NORTH EAST LINCOLNSHIRE COUNCIL	
01021755	
Bertrams	11/02/2013
ROM	£13.50

For Lucy Gilmour,
a very special editor,
with love and thanks for everything. X

CHAPTER ONE

I WAS having a good day until George Challoner turned up.

It had rained almost every day since I had arrived in Yorkshire, but that morning I woke to a bright, breezy day. By some miracle Audrey had started first time, and I hummed as I drove along the country lanes lined with jaunty daffodils to Whellerby Hall.

When I arrived at the site, Frank, the lugubrious foreman, had even smiled—a first. Well, his face relaxed slightly in response to my cheery greeting, but in my current mood I was prepared to count it a smile. Progress, anyway.

The ready-mixed concrete arrived bang on time. I stood and watched carefully as the men started pouring it into the reinforced steel raft for the foundations. They clearly knew what they were doing, and I had already checked the quality of the concrete. After a frenzied couple of weeks, I could tell Hugh that the project was back on schedule.

Phew.

Everything was going to plan. I had it all worked out.

1. Get site experience.
2. Get job overseas on major construction project.
3. Get promoted to senior engineer.

And because I was an expert planner, I had made sure all my goals were Specific, Measurable, Attainable, Realistic and Time-bound. I was aiming for promotion by the time I was thirty, an overseas job by the end of the year, and I was already getting site experience with the new conference and visitor centre on the Whellerby Hall estate.

True, things had got off to a shaky start. Endless rain, unreliable suppliers and a construction team made up of dour Yorkshiremen who had apparently missed out on a century of women's liberation and made no secret of their reluctance to take orders from a female. My attempts to involve them in team-building exercises had *not* gone down well.

For a while, I admit, I had wondered if I had made a terrible mistake leaving the massive firm in London, but my plan was clear. I badly needed some site experience, and the Whellerby project was too good an opportunity to miss.

And now it might all just be coming together, I congratulated myself, checking another grid off on my clipboard. I'd won a knock-down-drag-out fight with the concrete supplier, which might account for Frank's—sort of—smile and now we could start building.

Perhaps I could let myself relax, just a little.

That was when George arrived.

He drove the battered Land Rover as if it were a Lamborghini, swinging into the site and parking—deliberately squint, I was sure!—next to Audrey in a flurry of mud and gravel.

I pressed my lips together in disapproval. George Challoner was allegedly the estate manager, although as far as I could see this involved little more than turning up at inconvenient moments and distracting everyone else who was actually trying to do some work.

He was also my neighbour. I'd been delighted at first to

be given my own cottage on the estate. I was only working on the project until Hugh Morrison, my old mentor, had recovered from his heart attack, and I didn't want to get involved with expensive long-term lets so a tied cottage for no rent made perfect sense.

I was less delighted to discover that George Challoner lived on the other side of the wall, his cottage a mirror image of mine under a single slate roof. It wasn't that he was a noisy neighbour, but I was always so aware of him, and it wasn't because he was attractive, if that's what you're thinking.

I was prepared to admit that he was extremely easy on the eye. My own preference was for dark-haired men, while George was lean and rangy with hair the colour of old gold and ridiculously blue eyes, but, still, I could see that he was good-looking.

OK, he was *very* good-looking. *Too* good-looking.

I didn't trust good-looking men. I'd fallen for a dazzling veneer once before, and it wasn't a mistake I intended to make again.

I watched balefully as George waved and strode across to join me at the foundations. The men had all brightened at his approach and were shouting boisterous abuse at him. Even Frank grinned, the traitor.

I sighed. What was it with men? The ruder they were, the more they seemed to like each other.

'Hey, Frank, don't look now but your foundations are full of holes,' said George, peering down at the steel cages.

'They're supposed to be that way,' I said, even though I knew he was joking. I hated the way George always made me feel buttoned-up. 'The steel takes the tensile stress.'

'I wish I had something to take *my* stress,' said George. He had an irritating ability to give the impression that he was laughing while keeping a perfectly straight face.

Something to do with the glinting blue eyes, I thought, or perhaps the almost imperceptible deepening of the creases around his eyes. Or the smile that seemed to be permanently tugging at the corner of his mouth.

Whatever it was, I wished he wouldn't do it. It made me feel...ruffled.

Besides, I had never met anybody less stressed. George Challoner was one of those charmed individuals for whom life was a breezy business. He never seemed to take anything seriously. God only knew why Lord Whellerby had made him estate manager. I was sure George was just playing at it, amusing himself between sunning himself on the deck of a yacht or playing roulette in some swish casino.

I knew his type.

'What can we do for you, George?' I said briskly. 'As you can see, we're rather busy here today.'

'The guys are busy,' said George, nodding at the foundations where the men had gone back to pouring the concrete. 'You're just watching.'

'I'm *supervising*,' I said with emphasis. 'That's my job.'

'Good job, just watching everyone else do the work.'

I knew quite well that he was just trying to wind me up, but I ground my teeth anyway. 'I'm the site engineer,' I said. 'That means I have to make sure everything is done properly.'

'A bit like being an estate manager, you mean?' said George. 'Except you get to wear a hard hat.'

'I don't see that my job has anything in common with yours,' I said coldly. 'And talking of hard hats, if you must come onto the site, you should be wearing one. I've reminded you about that before.'

George cast a look around the site. Beyond the foundations where the concrete mixer churned, it was a sea of mud. It had been cleared the previous autumn and was now littered with machinery and piles of reinforcing wires. 'I'm taller than everything here,' he objected. 'I can't see a single thing that could fall on my head.'

'You could trip over and knock your head on a rock,' I said, adding under my breath, 'with any luck.'

'I heard that!' George grinned, and I clutched my clipboard tighter to my chest and put up my chin. 'I never had to wear a hard hat when Hugh Morrison was overseeing,' he said provocatively.

'That was before we'd started construction, and, in any case, that was up to Hugh. This is my site now, and I like to follow correct procedures.'

I promise you, I wasn't always unbearably pompous, but there was just something about George that rubbed me up the wrong way.

'Now, that's a useful thing to know,' he exclaimed. 'Maybe that's where I've been going wrong!'

His gaze rested on my face. Nobody had the right to have eyes that blue, I thought crossly as I fought the colour that was stealing along my cheekbones. My fine, fair skin was the bane of my life. The slightest thing and I'd end up blushing like a schoolgirl.

'So what's the correct procedure for asking you out?' he asked, leaning forward confidentially as if he really expected me to tell him.

I kept my composure. Making a big play of looking over at the foundations and then checking something off my list, I said coolly: 'You ask me out, and I say no.'

'I've tried that,' he objected.

He had. The first night I arrived, he had popped round to suggest a drink at the pub in the village. He asked me every time he saw me. I was sure it was just to annoy me now. Any normal man would have got the point by then.

'Then I'm not sure what I can suggest.'

'Come on, we're neighbours,' said George. 'We should be friendly.'

'It's precisely *because* we're neighbours that I don't think it's a good idea,' I said, making another mark on my clipboard. George wasn't to know it was meaningless. 'You live right next door to me. If we went for a drink and you turned out to be some kind of weirdo, I'd never be able to get away from you.'

'Weirdo?'

He was doing his best to sound outraged, but he didn't fool me. I could tell he was trying not to laugh.

Pushing my hair behind my ears, I glared at him.

'Maybe weirdo isn't quite the right word,' I allowed, 'but you know what I mean.'

'I see.' George pretended to ponder. 'So you think that after one date, I might never leave you alone? I might pester you to go out again or fall madly in love with you?'

My beastly cheeks were turning pink again, I could feel it. 'I don't think that's very likely.'

'Why not?'

I looked down at my clipboard, wishing that he would stop asking awkward questions and just go away.

'I'm not the kind of girl men fall madly in love with,' I said evenly after a moment.

Sadly, all too true.

George pursed his lips and his eyes danced. 'OK, so if you're not worried about me falling for you, maybe you're worried *you'll* fall madly in love with *me*.'

'I can assure you *that's* not going to happen!' I snapped.

'That sounds like a challenge to me.'

'It certainly isn't,' I said. 'I'm just saying that you're not my type.'

Of course, he couldn't leave it there, could he? 'What *is* your type, then?'

'Not you, anyway,' I told him firmly, and he put on an injured look. Like I say, he didn't take anything seriously.

'Why not?'

'I don't trust handsome men,' I said. 'You're too good-looking for me.'

'Hey, isn't that lookist or something?' he protested. 'You wouldn't hold my looks against me if I was ugly, would you? Or at least you wouldn't admit it.'

I sighed. 'I don't know why you're so keen to ask me out anyway,' I said. 'You must be desperate for a date.'

'I'm just trying to be friendly.'

'Well, I appreciate it,' I said crisply, 'but I'm only here for a couple of months and I'd rather keep our relationship professional if that's all right with you.'

'I like the idea of us having a relationship,' said George, 'but I'm not so sure about the professional bit. Is everything professional with you, Frith?'

'It is while I'm here. This job is important to me,' I told him. 'I really needed some site experience and this is my first time in charge. It's a great chance for me. Plus, this contract is really important to Hugh. He's been so good to me, I don't want to let him down.'

I looked around the site, narrowing my eyes as I envisaged what the centre would look like when it was finished. The specifications were for the use of sustainable materials wherever possible, and the wood and glass finish was designed to blend into the backdrop of the trees edging the site.

'It's going to look good,' I told George. 'It's expensive, but I gather Lord Whellerby's plan is to make Whellerby Hall the top conference venue in the north, and the centre will be a step towards that. It's a good idea,' I added. I rather liked the sound of Lord Whellerby. I hadn't met him yet, but I got the impression that he was astute and sensible—unlike his estate manager!

George had been following my gaze, rocking back on his heels as he studied the site thoughtfully. The breeze ruffled his hair and set it glinting where it caught the sunlight. In spite of the muddy boots and worn Guernsey, he looked as if he were modelling for a country sports catalogue.

'He had to do something,' he said frankly. 'These stately homes are expensive to keep up. Roly nearly passed out when he saw the first heating bill!'

'Does Lord Whellerby know you call him Roly?' I asked disapprovingly. In spite of his regular requests for progress reports, he had never visited the site, apparently happy to appoint the laid-back George as his go-between.

'We were at school together,' George said. 'He's lucky if Roly is all I call him!'

'Oh.' I was disconcerted. 'I'd imagined an older man.'

'No, he's thirty-two. He never expected to inherit Whellerby. The last Lord Whellerby was his great-uncle, and he had a son and a grandson who were groomed to take over the estate in due course. But they had a whole string of family tragedies and Roly was pitched into the middle of things.'

'It must have been difficult for him,' I said, still trying to picture Lord Whellerby as a young man instead of the experienced landowner I'd imagined.

'It was. This is a big estate. It was a lot to take on, and Roly had never even lived in the country before. He had no experience and he was frankly terrified. I don't blame him,' said George.

'Oh.' The breeze was pushing in some clouds, I noticed worriedly. It kept blowing my hair around my face and I wished I'd taken the time to plait it. My hair, by the way, is another bane of my life. It is fine and straight and brown and I can't do anything with it other than let it hang there.

I pulled away a strand that had plastered itself against my lips, still trying to reconfigure this new information about Lord Whellerby, who was, after all, the client.

'Did you come here at the same time?' I asked George.

'Not immediately. Roly inherited an estate manager from his great-uncle and the guy was running rings round him. I was…at a loose end, shall we say? Roly invited me up to keep him company for a while, and when the estate manager left he asked if I wanted the job.' George grinned and spread his hands. 'I had nothing better to do, so here I am.'

That rang true. George was exactly the kind of person who would get a job because of *who* he knew rather than *what* he knew, I thought darkly.

'Jobs for the boys, in fact?'

George's smile was easy. 'No one else would employ me,' he said, clearly unfazed by my disapproval.

I sniffed. 'I still think you should show your employer some respect and refer to him as Lord Whellerby,' I said primly.

'Do you call Hugh Mr Morrison?'

'That's different.'

'How?'

'He's not a lord, for a start.'

George made a big deal of shaking his head and then smacking his ear as if to clear it. 'Sorry, that was really weird,' he told her. 'For a minute there I thought we were in the twenty-first century, but, thank God, we're back in the nineteenth where we all know our place!'

'Maybe it *is* old-fashioned of me,' I conceded, 'but I happen to think there's nothing wrong with using a title to show a bit of respect.'

'You call me George.'

'And your point is…?'

He raised his hands in surrender and smiled. 'I'd hate to be called Mr Challoner, anyway,' he said. 'I'd constantly be looking over my shoulder for my father.' For a second, his mouth was set and a grimness touched his eyes, but so fleetingly that afterwards I decided that I must have imagined it.

A moment later, and the blue eyes were full of laughter once more. As they rested on my face I realised just how long I had been standing and talking to him when I should have been overseeing the pouring of the concrete.

'Look, did you want something in particular?' I said, summoning my best crisp manner. 'Because I really do need to get on.'

'I'm on my way up to the Hall. I just thought I'd drop by and see how things were going so I can give Roly—excuse me, Lord Whellerby—an update.'

'I've done a progress report if he'd like one.'

'Another one?'

'I got the impression Lord Whellerby likes to be kept informed,' I said stiffly. 'It's part of my job to keep the client happy.'

'I must remember to tell Roly that,' said George with a wink, which I met with a stony look.

'Would he like this report or not?'

'Oh, absolutely.'

'Fine.' Tucking my clipboard under my arm, I shouted to Frank over the sound of the concrete mixer. 'Can you carry on, Frank?' I pointed at the clouds. 'And keep an eye on those!'

Frank lifted a hand in acknowledgement and I led the way to the site office. I don't know if you've ever tried it, but there is no way to walk gracefully through mud in a pair of Wellington boots. The mud sucked at my feet and made horrible squelching sounds, and I was horribly aware of George behind me, watching me waddle. I had to resist the urge to tug my safety jacket further down over my rear.

'Boots,' I said, pointing to George's feet when we reached the prefabricated building that housed the site office, and he threw a crisp salute. Needless to say, he had made it across the mud as if he were walking across a perfectly mown lawn.

I ignored him. My boots were so clogged with mud that I struggled to get them off even using the scraper at the bottom of the steps, but after a tussle that George watched with undisguised amusement I managed to replace them with a pair of pumps I kept just inside the door. Tossing my hard hat onto a chair, I stalked across to my computer and pulled up the file, my colour still high.

George—of course—had no trouble taking off his own boots. He lounged in the doorway in his socks while I bent over the printer and concentrated fiercely on the pages spewing out. I could feel his eyes on me, and I plucked at the collar of the simple blue shirt I was wearing, wishing I could blame the single electric radiator for the warmth climbing into my cheeks.

Collecting up the pages, I banged them neatly together on the desk and fastened them with a bang of the stapler. 'There you go.'

'Thanks.'

But instead of leaving, George threw himself down in the visitor's chair on the other side of the desk and flicked through the pages. 'I see you've changed the specifications for the storm water drainage system,' he said, then he glanced up at my face. 'What?' he said.

'Nothing. I was just…surprised.'

'What, you thought I couldn't read a report?'

'Of course not.' I tugged at my shirt front. The truth was that I had assumed that he was too laid-back to pick up on the details of the report. 'You don't strike me as a details person, that's all.'

A faint smile curled his mouth. 'I can pay attention when required,' he said.

'Right.' I cleared my throat. 'Well, as you've noted, I'm putting in a different kind of underground chamber to store the rainwater run-off. I think this one is a better design.'

'More expensive though,' George commented, flicking through to the figures.

'It is, but we're saving money with a better deal on the glass wool cavity insulation slabs. If you look at the last page, you'll see we're still on target to stick to the budget.'

'Good. We can't—' George broke off as a disembodied voice started shouting:

HEY, YOUR PHONE IS RINGING! PICK UP THE PHONE! YES, YOU, IT'S YOUR PHONE. DON'T EVEN TRY AND IGNORE IT! PICK IT UP RIGHT NOW!

He laughed at my expression. 'Good, isn't it?'

Embarrassed at having jumped so obviously, I smoothed back my hair. 'Hilarious,' I said, watching as George extracted the still-squawking phone from his pocket. I always leapt to answer my phone, but George only studied the screen in a leisurely manner, apparently able to ignore the noise it was making.

'It's Roly,' he said. 'Wonder what he wants?'

ANSWER THE PHONE! PICK UP THE PHONE! It wasn't often that I found myself in agreement with an object.

'Crazy idea, I know, but you could try answering it and find out,' I suggested acidly.

George only grinned as he pressed the answer button. 'Yes, my lord?' The comment at the other end made him laugh. 'I understand I'm not showing you enough respect,' he explained, waggling his eyebrows at me. I tucked in the corners of my mouth and refused to respond.

Irritably, I began straightening the already immaculately aligned files set out in order of priority. I had phone calls to make of my own, but how could I concentrate when George was leaning back in the chair, tipping back dangerously as he yakked on to Lord Whellerby?

'*Who*?' he said suddenly, letting the chair crash forwards in his surprise. 'You're kidding! What's *she* doing there?' A pause as he listened, his eyebrows climbing towards his hairline. 'Yes… Yes, it is… Her what?'

I shifted uneasily as the blue eyes focused on my face. 'You're kidding!' he said again, looking at me so strangely that I mouthed *What?* at him. 'Yes…yes…I'll tell her. See you in a bit.'

George snapped the phone back and stared at me.

'What?' I said out loud.

'You've heard of Saffron Taylor?' he said conversationally, and a dreadful feeling of foreboding stole over me.

'Omigod,' I said in a sinking voice.

'Adored daughter of charismatic tycoon Kevin Taylor? The ultimate IT girl? Darling of the celebrity circuit?'

'Omigod,' I said again.

'She's crying in Roly's private sitting room.'

I stared at him, aghast. 'Omigod!' It was all I could say.

'And she *says* she's your sister.'

I dropped my head in my hands. 'Please tell me this is a joke! Saffron can't be here. She gets disorientated if she leaves Knightsbridge!'

'*Saffron Taylor* is your sister?'

'OK.' I lifted my head and set my palms flat on the desk. Drawing a deep breath in through my nose, I exhaled slowly. 'Random sister in client's house. No need to panic.'

'She *is* your sister!'

'Half-sister,' I said, rummaging in my bag for Audrey's keys. 'What in God's name is she doing at Whellerby Hall?'

'Crying, I think.'

A thought zoomed in out of nowhere and hit me so hard I almost buckled at the knees. 'Has something happened to my father?'

God, what if something had happened to him? My mind spun frantically. What would I do? What would I say? What would I *feel*?

'I think we'd have heard on the news if something had happened to Kevin Taylor,' said George in a practical voice and I clutched at the thought.

'Yes, yes, you're right!' I said gratefully.

'Roly said something about a wedding, I think,' he went on. 'But he was whispering, so I might have got that wrong.'

I clutched my hair. 'Please don't tell me Saffron has come all the way up here because of some *wedding* crisis!'

'I gather she wanted to talk to you.'

'Then why didn't she just ring? Oh!' A horrible thought struck me. Another one. I pulled out my phone and stared at its blank screen. 'I switched my phone off last night,' I remembered in a hollow voice.

'I always find it helps to keep my phone on if I want people to get in touch with me,' said George, but I was in too much of a fret to rise to his smug tone.

'I've just had so many phone calls from Saffron about the wedding,' I said as I switched on the phone. 'It's been going on for months already. Which superstar rock band should be flown in to perform? Should she get her dress designed in New York or Paris or London? Castle A will look better in the photos, but castle B has a helipad, so which should she choose? It's totally out of control!'

My phone began beeping as message after message came through. Distractedly, I scrolled through the ream of texts.

'Call me… Call me… Crisis… Where r u?…I need u,' I read. 'Good grief, what's been going on?'

'Perhaps you'd better see her and find out.'

'I would if I could just find my *car key*!' I went back to scrabbling in the depths of my bag. 'I know it's in here!'

George got to his feet. 'I'll give you a lift, if you like. I'm going up to the Hall anyway.'

He was really enjoying the fact that I was so flustered, I could tell. The moment I knew Saffron was all right, I was going to kill her, I thought vengefully.

'There's really no need—ah!' My fingers closed around the car key at last and I pulled it triumphantly out of my bag. 'Here it is. I'll be fine, thanks.'

I hurried down the steps and hop-skip-jumped my way around the puddles to Audrey while George was putting on his boots.

'I'll tell Frank you'll be a while, shall I?'

Oh, God, I'd forgotten about the foundations! I dithered desperately as I hung onto the driver's door. I needed to be on site, but I couldn't leave my sister weeping all over my client. I hated being beholden to George Challoner, but I didn't have time to explain to Frank now.

'Er, yes…thank you,' I said. 'If you wouldn't mind.'

'Sure.'

He strolled over to the foundations while I flung myself into Audrey and shoved the key in the ignition.

Audrey wheezed, coughed, managed a splutter and then died.

I made myself breathe slowly. My sister was having hysterics over the client who was key to the success of Hugh's business. I mustn't panic. I would deal with it the way I dealt with everything else, firmly and capably. All I had to do was to apologise to Lord Whellerby and remove Saffron.

No problem.

Except that Audrey had chosen now not to cooperate. I tried to start the engine again, but got only more wheezing, feebler this time.

More deep breaths. I counted to ten and then turned the ignition key once more.

'*Please*, Audrey,' I muttered, jaw clenched. I was acutely aware of George Challoner, who had delivered the message to Frank and was now watching me from behind the wheel of the Land Rover. 'Don't let me down,' I begged Audrey. 'Not when *he's* watching.'

But Audrey did.

One last turn of the ignition key, and not even a wheeze in return.

I resisted the urge to bang my head against the steering wheel. Just.

I couldn't sit there any longer. I knew what Saffron was like when she got in a state, and if Lord Whellerby was anything like every other man I had known, he would be terrified. He was probably already Googling for another design and build company to complete his conference centre, I thought bitterly.

How was I going to explain *that* to Hugh?

I know this was the big contract to ensure the future of your company, but, see, Saffron was having a bit of a crisis and now we've lost the contract? I'd be lucky if Hugh didn't have another heart attack.

Barely two weeks on the job, and what would I have to show for it? Hugh back in hospital, out of a job, my best chance for site experience blown. My plan would be in tatters, my career would be over before it had really begun.

I pulled myself up short. Good grief, I was getting as bad as Saffron! There was no point in overreacting until I knew what the situation was, and to do that I had to get to Whellerby Hall.

My eyes flickered to George, and then away.

I could walk to the Hall, but it would take too long to cross the estate.

There was only one thing to be done.

Sucking in a breath, I got out of Audrey, closed the door, walked deliberately around the bonnet of the Land Rover and got in next to George without a word.

For a moment I sat there, looking straight through the windscreen, my lips pressed so firmly together they almost disappeared.

'Thank you,' I said at last, forcing the words out. 'I'd be very glad of a lift.'

'My pleasure,' said George.

To my annoyance, his engine leapt into life without so much as a murmur of protest. I cast a reproachful look at Audrey as George reversed out behind her, and changed gear.

'You know, you could invest in a reliable car,' he said, a ghost of amusement in his voice.

'I couldn't get rid of Audrey,' I said, instantly on the defensive. 'She's a great car. It's just that she can be a little... temperamental.'

Or downright contrary, at times.

George raised an eyebrow. Have you ever met anyone who could actually do that? Raise one brow? George could.

'*Audrey*?' he said.

'She's named after Audrey Hepburn. Because she's so glamorous,' I added when George seemed unable to make the connection.

'Right.' He glanced at me and then away, shaking his head a little, but I could see the curl at the corner of his mouth.

I pushed my seat belt into place with a firm click. 'She's

got style,' I said defiantly. Vintage, perhaps, but definitely style.

'Lime green is an interesting choice of colour,' George commented.

'It's not everyone's first choice, I know,' I said, 'but she was the only car I could afford when I bought her. I washed dishes for three years to pay for a car of my own,' I told George. 'Audrey's a symbol as much as a car.'

George swung the Land Rover out of the site gates and onto one of the narrow lanes that criss-crossed the Whellerby estate. 'I'm surprised to hear Kevin Taylor's daughter had to buy her own car,' he said. 'Wouldn't your father buy you one? It's not like he can't afford it.'

My face closed down the way it always did when I had to talk about my father. I hugged my arms together and looked out of the window. I hadn't taken a penny from him since I left school, and I wasn't about to start now.

'I pay my own way,' I said. 'I always have, and I always will.'

CHAPTER TWO

'I DIDN'T even know Kevin Taylor had another daughter,' said George.

I kept my eyes on the hedgerow brushing past my window. 'Few people do,' I said. My voice was perfectly even, the way I had trained it to be when I talked about my father. 'I'm not sure he even knows himself any more.'

'How long is it since you've seen him?'

'Six years. I made the mistake of asking if he'd come to my graduation,' I said. 'He went to New York on business instead.'

As soon as I said it, I regretted it. I couldn't think what had possessed me to tell George Challoner of all people about that bitter memory. I tensed, waiting for the sympathetic noises, but he surprised me.

'I haven't seen my parents for four years,' he said, and I slewed round in my seat to look at him in surprise. He was so golden, so effortlessly charming. I couldn't imagine him falling out with anyone.

'Why not?'

'We had an…er…disagreement,' he said, lifting one hand from the steering wheel and spreading it in an eloquent gesture of resignation. 'It culminated in one of those never-darken-our-doorstep-again conversations, and so I haven't.'

'I know what those are like,' I said, unprepared to find myself sharing some fellow feeling with George.

'Fun, aren't they?'

'Fabulous,' I agreed. 'Can't get enough of them.'

'Still, at least you've got your sister,' said George. 'I did family estrangement as a job lot. I haven't seen my brother since then either.' He spoke lightly, but I sensed the pain lurking, and I looked away.

'Perhaps I should be grateful for Saffron, then,' I said, keeping my tone light to match his. 'Although if she upsets Lord Whellerby and anything goes wrong with Hugh's contract, I will personally strangle her and then I'll end up without any family either.'

'Don't worry about Roly,' said George reassuringly. 'He's really not the grudge-bearing type.'

'I hope you're right.' I gnawed fretfully at my thumbnail.

'Is your sister really going to marry Jax Jackson?' George asked to distract me after a moment.

'Half-sister,' I said automatically. 'And so she says. I'm not really sure what it's all about,' I confessed, shifting back with a sigh to look out of my window where the hedgerows were a blur of spring green.

'As far as I can tell Jax was a mediocre pop star until he started dating Saffron and became a celebrity. Now he's on the cover of all those glossy magazines you get at the checkout in the supermarket. He seems to spend most of his time on tour, but Saffron's so thrilled by the idea of getting married that he appears to be incidental to the whole process.

'It's going to be the wedding of the century, I gather,' I added with a sigh. Ever since Saffron had announced her engagement, she had been in a frenzy of wedding plans, and if I never heard the word wedding again right then, I'd have been more than happy.

George glanced at me. 'So are you going to be brides-maid?'

'No, thank God. Saffron did ask me, but obviously only because she thought she should, and when I said I didn't think I'd fit with her other bridesmaids and would rather just be happy for her on the sidelines, she was so relieved it was funny. I really don't blend with Saffron's décor,' I said to George. 'She's a socialite and I'm an engineer...you can probably imagine how much we have in common!'

'I'd certainly never have guessed you were sisters,' he agreed. 'You don't look at all alike.'

'No, Saffron's gorgeous,' I said without rancour. 'Her mother was a model, and Saffron gets her looks from her, not my father. Saffron's blonde and bubbly and beautiful, and I'm...not.'

I wasn't looking at George, but I could feel the blue eyes on my profile. Instinctively, I lifted my chin a little higher to show him that I didn't care.

'No one could argue that you were blonde,' he said. 'And I'd put you down as prickly rather than bubbly, but other-wise I think you underestimate yourself.'

'You don't need to be polite,' I said, in what he probably thought was a very prickly way. 'I know I'm not beautiful. I'm not ugly either. I'm just...ordinary. As my father never tired of telling people when I was younger, Saffron got the beauty, and I got the brains.'

'Ouch.'

'It's true.' I shrugged. 'Saffron and I are so different it's almost comical when we're together, which isn't very often.'

'And yet it's you she rings when she's upset.'

'That's because she doesn't have a mother. Tiffany ran off with her personal trainer when Saffron was a baby, and she died a couple of years after that. I always felt sorry for Saffron. She was the prettiest little girl, and she's always been the apple of my father's eye, but nobody really had any time for her.'

'So you're the big sister?'

'That's right. I was seven when my father decided a model suited his image better than my mother. Mum didn't want a divorce, but when Tiffany got pregnant, Dad insisted. His company wasn't as successful as it is now, so the settlement was fairly modest, and Mum and I had a very ordinary life. We lived in the suburbs and I went to the local school.

'It was fine,' I said, pushing away the memory of my mother weeping at night when she thought I couldn't hear her. It hadn't been fine for her. 'But I had to spend two weeks every summer with my father, who was super rich by then and kept getting richer. It was like being dropped into a whole different world. I hated it,' I said.

I sighed. 'And then Mum died when I was fifteen.'

'I'm sorry,' George said, all traces of his usual lurking smile gone. 'That must have been hard for you.'

'It was awful.' I pressed my lips together in a straight line. Just thinking about that time could still send a wave of desolation crashing over me.

Mum was only thirty-nine when she dropped dead at the sink one day. 'The doctors said it was an embolism, and that she wouldn't have felt a thing. I wasn't there,' I told George. 'I was at school, and a neighbour found her. By the time I got home, they had taken Mum away.'

I swallowed hard, remembering how I had stood in the kitchen in dazed disbelief. One minute my mother had been there, the next she wasn't. Gone, just like that.

There was nothing I could have done, even if I had been there. Everybody said so. But deep down, I always felt as if I should have known. I should have said goodbye and told her I loved her instead of cramming a piece of toast in my mouth and running for the bus. I wish I could remember the last thing I said to her, but I can't. It was just an ordinary day.

And then it wasn't.

'My whole world fell apart.' I'd almost forgotten that I was talking to George by then.

My nice safe life had vanished the moment that clot blocked my mother's brain and I was pitched into an existence where nothing seemed certain any more. For months I flailed around in a hopeless search for something to hold onto, until I realised one day that the only thing I could be sure of was myself.

Slowly, carefully, I built a new life, and I made it as secure as I could. Friends sighed and called me a control freak, and maybe I was, but routines and plans at least gave me a structure, one that nobody else could take away from me without warning. Without them, I would have been lost.

'Presumably you went to live with your father then?' said George after a moment.

'If you can call being packed off to boarding school "living" with him,' I said. 'At least I had Saffron in the holidays. She's over seven years younger than me, but neither of us had a mother and she was so desperate for attention that we used to spend a lot of time together then.

'It was Saffron who painted the eyelashes over Audrey's headlights,' I told George.

'I wondered about that.'

'She was so pleased with them, I didn't have the heart to paint them out, and now they're part of her.' My smile was probably a little twisted. 'Saffron's spoilt, but she's got a sweet nature and all she wants is a little attention. Unfortunately, this wedding has made her hysterical.' I sighed, remembering the situation. 'I just hope Lord Whellerby's not too angry.'

'You haven't met Roly yet, have you? If you had, you'd know you've got nothing to worry about,' said George when I shook my head.

'Easy for you to say,' I said tensely. 'It's not your sister having hysterics over your most important client!'

We were bowling up an avenue lined with stately trees. To either side stretched lush parklands, with placid cows grazing under the horse chestnuts. The Land Rover rattled over a cattle grid, the avenue curved round over a hill, and I caught my first sight of Whellerby Hall. I'd been too busy to visit before, and my jaw dropped.

It was an extravaganza of a house, a vast Baroque structure with a domed roof in the centre, and two wings stretching out on either side, set atop a slope on the far side of a serene lake.

George drove right up to the imposing entrance and parked with a crunch of gravel. The door was opened by a cadaverous-looking individual who looked offended by George's cheerfully casual greeting but unbent enough to explain that Lord Whellerby was in his private sitting room.

'That's Simms.' George led the way up a sweeping marble staircase, past massive oil paintings of naval battles and skimpily clad nymphs. My father's house was ostentatiously ornate, but still I had to make an effort not to goggle at the sheer size of the Hall. 'He was old Lord Whellerby's butler, and Roly inherited him along with the house. Roly's terrified of him.'

'I don't blame him.'

'You'd get on well with Simms. He always refers to Roly as Lord Whellerby too. He'd really like Roly to be out shooting peasants all day and coming home to sit over his port and cigars.'

'It's a strange way to live, isn't it?' I said as we climbed another flight of stairs, rather less imposing this time.

'I know. I feel as if I'm part of a costume drama whenever I come to see Roly. I keep expecting a dowager duchess to pop up and tick me off for seducing the housemaids under the stairs—and no, before you ask,' he said, turning his head with a smile that did odd things to my breathing. 'There are no maids. A very efficient cleaning firm comes in once a week, and they're far too busy to dally with me anywhere.'

'Disappointing for you,' I said tartly to cover the fact that my lungs were still not cooperating with the business of inflating and deflating. Perhaps it was all these stairs, I thought hopefully. George *was* taking them awfully fast. It was hard to believe a single smile could have such an effect.

'Not at all. I'm fussy about who I dally with,' said George. 'I like a challenge,' he said, turning his head to look straight at me. 'I like to be intrigued. I like classy girls who don't need me and maybe don't even like me. I like to feel that any dallying I do will lead to something really…special.'

I waited for him to smile to show me that he was joking, but he didn't. He just kept looking into my eyes and for some reason my breathing got all tangled up again.

So, nothing to do with his smile. Must be those stairs after all.

'Here we are.' A minute or so later, when we had trekked down a long corridor, and I had given up trying to work out whether or not he had been serious, George flung open a door. 'Frith to the rescue,' he announced.

There was a moment of silence in the room, and then both occupants of a sofa leapt to their feet.

I had a professional smile fixed on my face to greet Lord Whellerby, but Saffron gave me no chance to make the flu-

ent apology I had planned. She stumbled across the room
to throw herself into my arms. 'Oh, Frith,' she wailed. 'I'm
so glad to see you! Everything's gone so horribly wrong!'

I held her close and patted her back comfortingly, while
trying to grimace apologetically over her shoulder at Lord
Whellerby, who was hovering anxiously. I could see why
George had been amused when I insisted on referring to
him as Lord Whellerby. He had a pleasant face, fair skin
that clearly flushed as easily as mine, a solid figure that was
already growing stout and a hesitant air in marked contrast
to George's easy assurance.

I could feel George watching us, and, although I couldn't
see his face, I knew that his eyes would be dancing. We
must have looked ridiculous. Saffron was so much taller
than I was, she had to bend right over to bury her head on
my shoulder. She was shuddering with little sobs and clearly
teetering on the edge of hysterics. That was all I needed.

'That's enough, Saffron,' I said sharply. 'Stop crying
and tell me what you're doing here.'

My sister is one of those irritating women who can cry
prettily. When I held her away from me, tears spangled
the end of her beautiful green eyes, and her soft mouth
trembled, but under my stern gaze she made an effort to
gulp back her tears and bravely knuckled beneath her eyes,
being careful, I noted, not to smudge any of her mascara.

Roly—impossible to think of him as anything else
now!—hovered nearby, clearly torn between relief that
Saffron had stopped crying at last and alarm at my crisp
approach.

'I had to s-see you,' Saffron hiccupped. 'Daddy's in
Beijing and there's no one else.'

'What's the matter?' She really did seem upset, I thought
with compunction. Perhaps there was something really
wrong. 'Is it Jax?'

'No.' The beautiful face crumpled and Saffron buried her head back on my shoulder. 'It's Buffy!'

'Buffy?' I echoed blankly. 'Who's Buffy?'

'My bridesmaid! My *chief* bridesmaid! She's ruined *everything*!'

Another outburst of weeping. Roly wrung his hands helplessly, and I began to feel a little frayed at the edges.

'What on earth has this Buffy done?'

'She's getting married!'

George was grinning. He thought this was funny! I glared at him as I mentally counted to ten.

'OK, look, I'm sure we can sort this out, Saffron,' I said, keeping my voice calm, 'but not here. We'll go back to my cottage, I'll make you a cup of tea, and it'll all be fine.'

'What c-cottage?' sobbed Saffron.

'The cottage where I *live*,' I said with emphasis, and Saffron lifted her head, momentarily distracted from whatever crisis had been precipitated by the unknown Buffy.

'I thought you said you were living at Whellerby Hall?'

'I said I *worked* on the estate.' I drew a calming breath. 'This is Lord Whellerby's home and we're intruding.'

'Oh…really…no problem…'

'Who's Lord Whellerby?' Saffron's puzzled question broke over Roly's inarticulate stammer.

For answer, I turned her to face Roly, who shifted from foot to foot and blushed painfully.

'Oh, you should have told me!' Saffron gazed at him, her eyes still swimming with tears. 'You've been so sweet to me, too.'

'Pleasure,' he muttered, embarrassed. 'Please, call me Roly…er…I mean…' He lost himself in a morass of pleasantries.

I suppressed a sigh. This wasn't how I had imagined my client! But somehow I had to retrieve something from the situation. I hadn't wanted to meet him this way, but I would just have to make the best of it.

Tugging my jacket into place, I stepped forward and offered my hand. 'I'm so sorry about the misunderstanding, Lord Whellerby,' I said briskly, avoiding George's amused gaze. 'I'm Frith Taylor, the site engineer—and Saffron's sister, as you've obviously gathered.'

'Er…delighted.' Roly looked daunted by my formality, but he shook my hand.

'Thank you for looking after Saffron,' I went on. 'We'll get out of your way now.'

'Oh, but there's no n-need to go just y-yet,' said Roly, dismayed. 'Stay and, er, have some coffee or something.'

'That's very kind of you,' I said firmly, 'but we've imposed enough. Come along, Saffron,' I added to my sister, who was drawing shuddery little breaths and wiping tears pitifully from her cheeks with the back of her hand.

'It's starting to rain.' Roly dug in his pocket and produced a handkerchief, which he offered to Saffron, while my eyes flew to the window in consternation.

Sure enough, the clouds I'd told Frank to watch out for had grown into a threatening mass, and a sulky drizzle was already smearing the panes of the elegant windows.

Roly didn't care about my foundations. 'You've been so upset,' he told her. 'Sit and have something warm to drink before you go out in the cold,' he said, ignoring the tray of coffee that they had been drinking before George and I arrived.

Saffron took the handkerchief with a tremulous smile and dabbed at her cheeks with it. 'You're so kind,' she whispered, and Roly swelled with pleasure.

Oh, please, I thought, and caught George's eye. His expression was perfectly straight, but his blue eyes brimmed with amusement.

'I really don't think you should go out just yet,' Roly was saying. 'Now that your sister is here, you'll feel better. I'm sure she won't mind staying a bit longer and perhaps we can all help you resolve your problem.'

I opened my mouth to object to the delay, but George got in first. 'You may as well give in,' he murmured in my ear as Roly led Saffron tenderly back to the sofa. 'Once Roly starts stringing together real sentences, there'll be no budging him.'

'But the foundations—'

'You want to keep your client happy, don't you? I'll organise coffee and you see if you can find out why the diabolical Buffy's marriage has thrown her into disarray.'

So I found myself sitting on the sofa opposite my sister and my client, keeping a fretful eye on the rain, while Saffron, tears miraculously dried now that she had everyone fussing around her, lapped up Roly's admiration.

'I'm *so* sorry to cause all this trouble,' she was saying, her eyes wide and green. I have green eyes too, as a matter of fact, but mine are the ditchwater end of the spectrum while Saffron's are like the deep green of the Caribbean. Or so I've been told.

'I can't *tell* you how much better I feel! I was so upset last night, I couldn't sleep a wink. I couldn't get hold of Frith, and I really *needed* her, so in the end I just had to come and find her myself. It was quite an adventure.'

I frowned. 'How did you get here?' I asked, trying to imagine Saffron finding out about trains or looking at a map.

'Burke drove me.'

I should have known. Only Saffron would think being driven up the motorway in the back of luxurious limousine with tinted windows counted as an adventure.

'I had no idea it would be so *far*,' Saffron said and Roly gazed at her admiringly.

'You must be exhausted.'

'Oh, I am, but now that I'm here that doesn't matter.' Bravely, Saffron lifted her chin and managed a wobbly little smile.

Privately, I thought that my father's chauffeur was likely to be more tired than Saffron, but I knew better than to say so. I cast another glance at the window. For now the heavy rain was holding off, but I really needed to be on the site.

It was George who poured out the coffee when it arrived and passed around the cups. Then he sprawled in the corner of the sofa, one arm along the back, long legs stretched at an angle towards me. I perched at the other end, pretending not to notice that if I leant back he would be able to touch my shoulder. He'd hardly have to move at all to stroke my hair, or let his fingers drift along my jaw.

My pulse kicked a little just at the thought of it.

Annoyed with myself, I inched further along until I was pressed against the arm of the sofa. Why was I even thinking about George? I had more important problems to deal with.

'So, Saffron.' I cleared my throat and set my cup and saucer on the table between the two sofas. 'What exactly is the problem with Buffy?'

'She's not going to be here for my wedding!' said Saffron, eyes glistening with remembered outrage. 'She met this guy when she was skiing in Aspen earlier this year, and she thought it was just, like, a holiday romance, but yesterday he rang her and asked her to go back and marry him, and she's like, yes, I'm changing my life, so she's going next week.'

Crushed by the unfairness of it all, Saffron subsided back into the cushions, her beautiful mouth trembling.

'What a shame,' said Roly loyally and patted her hand.

I was irritatingly aware of George's hand just inches away. He was just sitting there, not doing anything but still making the air hum with an energy that made my scalp shrink alarmingly and raised the hairs on the back of my neck.

Not to mention making it almost impossible to concentrate.

'Well, that's OK, isn't it?' I had to feel my way cautiously. This wasn't quite how I had anticipated demonstrating my negotiating skills to the client, but Roly was paying close attention and was so obviously smitten with Saffron that I would have to be careful. 'I mean, it's quite romantic, isn't it?'

'What about my wedding? How am I going to manage without my chief bridesmaid?'

'Can't one of your other bridesmaids do it?' The last time I had been involved in exhaustive bridesmaid negotiations, Saffron had planned on at least six.

'There's no one suitable.'

I was losing patience. 'Being chief bridesmaid doesn't call for great management skills,' I said. 'It's not exactly life and death stuff, is it?'

A mistake. Saffron's emerald eyes flashed and she bounced up indignantly on the cushions. 'Are you saying my wedding's not important?'

'Well, it's not—' A casual nudge against my knee by George's foot made me pause, and realise that I was going about this quite the wrong way. 'I mean, of *course* it's important for you,' I amended with a quick glance at Roly. 'I just thought one of the other girls would do as well.'

It turned out that I had *no idea* what was involved in planning a wedding. Saffron enumerated all the chief bridesmaid's duties, ticking them off on her fingers, until

I was lost in details of fittings and favours and rehearsal dinners.

'And then, of course, there's the hen party,' said Saffron. 'That's nearly as important as the wedding itself. That's your main job.'

'Wait, hold on! *My* job?' I struggled forward on the sofa in consternation.

'You're the only one who can do it.'

'Oh, no. Oh, no, no, no, no.' I waved my hands frantically to push the very idea away. 'That's a very bad idea.'

George, the beast, was shaking with laughter. I could feel it reverberating along the sofa, and I glared at him.

'But you're my sister,' said Saffron, hurt.

'Saffron, we discussed this before, and we agreed I wouldn't fit in with everyone else.'

'And you're good at managing projects,' Saffron went on as if I hadn't spoken. 'It has to be you.'

I drew in a deep breath. I had to put a stop to this right away. 'I'm sorry,' I said as firmly as I knew how. 'I can't drop everything to run up and down to London, Saffron. I've got a visitor and conference centre to build on schedule and on budget...'

I stopped, realising that I might as well have been speaking Polish. It was doubtful if Saffron had ever come across the word 'budget' before.

'The thing is, Hugh's depending on me to see this project through for him,' I tried to explain. 'I can't let him down.'

'But you can let *me* down!'

Suppressing a sigh, I tried a different tack. 'You need a bridesmaid who can really give you the attention you deserve,' I said. 'One of your friends who lives in London and has the time to find you just the right place for your party, and help you choose all the wedding details. You know

I'm no good at that kind of thing,' I added with a cajoling smile, but Saffron refused to be consoled.

'You're my sister.' Saffron's lower lip trembled tragically. 'I'd think you'd *want* to be part of my big day. There's no one else I can rely on. Daddy's always working, and I've never had a mother.'

Saffron: barely a GCSE to her name, but a PhD in emotional blackmail.

'You've got Jax.'

'He's touring, and anyway he's no good at wedding stuff.' The green eyes swam with tears. Wordlessly, Roly reached for her hand, and Saffron permitted herself a little sob. 'Couldn't you at least organise the hen party? Otherwise I won't have one, and what sort of bride doesn't have a party?'

I drew a breath and told myself to stay firm. 'I would, but I have this pesky thing called a job. I realise you may not have come across the concept before,' I added, although the irony was lost on Saffron, 'but a job involves turning up at a specific time and place and working in exchange for money.'

'Well, that's not a problem. Daddy would pay you if you need money.'

My expression tightened. 'I'm not taking anything from him,' I said in a flat voice. 'And anyway, it's not about money. It's about responsibility. I've made a commitment to see this job through until Hugh is better. We have a contract and a responsibility to our client—who is Lord Whellerby here,' I said, not that I expected that to mean much to Saffron.

It was too much to hope that my sister might realise what an awkward situation she was putting me in and suddenly become rational.

Not that Roly was helping by patting Saffron's hand

sympathetically, as if her bridesmaid crisis were more important than getting his new conference centre built on time.

Saffron pouted. 'I don't see why you need a stupid job anyway. If you'd only talk to Daddy, you could do whatever you liked. I don't understand why you're both so stubborn about each other!'

'My career *is* what I like,' I said, exasperated. 'I don't understand why you can't understand *that*!'

'Then what am I going to do?' Saffron's face crumpled. 'Oh, I can't believe you'd be this mean to me!'

I rubbed my temples. I loved my sister, but sometimes she could be exasperating.

'I know the wedding is important to you, Saffron, but the conference centre is important to Lord Whellerby,' I said. 'A lot of money and a lot of jobs are depending on it, and the project has to come in on time.'

I threw an appealing look at Roly, who missed his cue completely. 'I'm sure a week or two late wouldn't matter,' he said, gazing adoringly at Saffron, who was making a great play of biting her lip while the tears trembled and sparkled bewitchingly on the ends of her lashes.

Helplessly, I turned without thinking to George. I don't know what my expression was like, but I must have seemed as if I was begging for help.

'I think it would matter to Hugh Morrison,' he said. 'It's not that long since his heart attack, and any delays would add a stress that he just doesn't need at the moment.'

'Exactly,' I said, with a grateful look, and Roly looked chastened.

Sensing that she was losing her support, Saffron slumped back. 'You don't seem to realise that organising a wedding is stressful too,' she complained. 'It's one of the most stressful times of your life, and that's why you need the support of your family. But if this Hugh person is more important to you than I am, I—'

George sat forward. 'Perhaps I could make a suggestion?'

I immediately looked wary, Saffron hopeful. 'What?' she asked tearfully.

'You want Frith to organise a bridal party for you, but she can't spare the time to go to London, right?' He waited for Saffron to nod, while my brows drew together suspiciously. 'So why not have the party here?' he said.

'*Here*?'

'Now I know what you're going to say.' George held up his hands to stop Saffron from going any further, focusing on her rather than on me, although he must have been able to feel me glaring at him from the other end of the sofa. 'You can't go clubbing in Whellerby. This isn't London, it isn't cool…but why not make your party different from all the others? Anyone can go to a club or a restaurant in London. How many people can take over a stately home?'

'Probably most of Saffron's friends,' I said crisply, my gratitude forgotten. I had a sinking suspicion where this was going. 'There's no question of—'

'You mean, like, a house party?' Saffron interrupted me.

'Exactly,' said George.

'We could wear costumes, like in that TV series…'

'You've got it. You could be the beautiful daughter, your friends can be dashing widows, or young ladies waiting to make their come out, and Frith could be the repressed housekeeper who's secretly in love with one of the footmen.'

'Hey—' I began, but Saffron was already clapping her hands.

'I love it! Think of the costumes! I've always wanted to wear one of those lovely evening gowns. I could wear long gloves!'

Buffy's treachery was forgotten. Saffron was positively bouncing on the sofa in excitement. 'Ooh, and we could make it a proper Edwardian house party...assignations in the conservatory, croquet on the lawn, dance cards...*dancing!*' Her eyes lit up as the idea caught hold. 'We could have a *ball*!'

'Now see what you've done,' I said to George with a severe look.

'We'll have to ask men too,' Saffron was bubbling on. 'We can't have a ball with just girls. But that's all right. Jax would look super hot in a DJ. A house like this must have a ballroom, right?'

I had heard enough. I held up my hands like a traffic cop. '*Stop!*' I said so forcefully that Saffron was startled into silence. 'Now just hold on a minute,' I said more calmly. 'We are not having a ball here. Or a dinner. Or anything at all. This is Lord Whellerby's home. It's not open to the public.'

'Yet,' said George.

'What?' I said, thrown by his calm interjection.

'The conference centre is just part of our strategy to turn Whellerby Hall into the leading venue for events in the north,' George said, with a glance at Roly, who nodded encouragement. 'Eventually, we'll turn the east wing into top-of-the-market accommodation for weddings and parties using the state rooms.'

'George says we'll be able to ch-charge an arm and a leg,' Roly confided.

'Of course, the east wing needs a lot of renovation before we can do that,' George added, 'but as that's the long-term plan, why don't we take advantage of Saffron's celebrity?'

My chest swelled with unreasonable resentment as he sat there, talking persuasively while Saffron and Roly lapped it up. I had had George down as a lightweight, a playboy down on his luck just playing at estate management. He wasn't supposed to be talking about strategies or long-term plans.

'You've both been too discreet to mention it,' he went on, 'but I think we all know how famous she is. Saffron Taylor is the ultimate party girl, and she's a social leader. Where she goes, others will follow.'

I closed my eyes in despair.

'We couldn't ask for better publicity. If Saffron and her closest friends have a private party up here, you can bet your bottom dollar everyone else will be clamouring to do the same. We don't need to do anything so vulgar as advertise. Word will get round—especially if we ask your friends not to give away the secret location of the party. Before we know where we are, we'll be beating people off with a stick.'

And so it was decided. I not only had to build a conference centre, I had to organise a costumed house party for a load of spoiled socialites.

I looked out of the window. It had started to rain in earnest.

CHAPTER THREE

'MAKE yourself at home, why don't you?' I dumped my briefcase on the worktop and raised my brows at George, who was leaning back in a chair with his feet on my kitchen table. And if I didn't very much mistake the matter, he was drinking my tea out of my mug.

'I knew you wouldn't mind,' he said with that smile that never failed to make my pulse kick, no matter how hard I braced myself against it. 'I've spent all afternoon talking about artificial insemination,' he said. 'I was desperate for a drink, but my fridge is empty, so I came to see what you had. All I could find was tea, though.'

'Oh, I'm sorry about that,' I said with mock contrition. 'I didn't realise that I had to keep a supply of booze in just in case you felt like dropping by.'

'You'll get used to country ways soon,' he said kindly, refusing to rise to my sarcasm. 'Some beers and a couple of bottles of wine are always good to have in stock. You never know who'll stop by.'

'Obviously,' I said. 'Is it a country way to break into other people's houses too?'

'I didn't break in. I used a key.'

'You know, it's a funny thing, but I could have sworn I locked the door when I left this morning,' I said.

'You did, and very sensible it was too, but I happen to

have a spare.' Extracting the key from his pocket, George waved it at me. 'There's always one next door in case you ever lose yours.'

'I'm always careful about my keys,' I said crushingly, and George studied me over the rim of his mug. My mug, rather.

'I get the impression you're careful about everything.'

'I find it easier that way,' I said.

Being careful had got me through after Mum had died. Being careful kept my life under control. Being careful kept me safe.

If I wasn't careful, I would find myself tumbling back into that abyss of grief and loneliness that it had taken such effort to climb out of all those years ago.

I had made a career out of being careful, in fact. I loved the precision of engineering, of putting exactly the right materials together in exactly the right way to build something solid and functional. Something that would stay where you left it and still be there when you went back at the end of the day.

Dropping into the chair across the table from him, I pushed my hair wearily behind my ears.

'Tired?'

'One of those days,' I said, 'and it didn't help that Saffron kept me up until the small hours yakking about how excited she was about the party. Thanks for that great idea!' I added sarcastically to George, who lifted the mug in acknowledgement.

'Anything to help.' He let his chair—my chair!—fall back to the floor. 'I'm sorry if Saffron got carried away, but it was a spur of the moment thing. You looked as if you could do with some support and it was the best I could think of.'

'An Edwardian-themed house party? I'd hate to hear how elaborate your well-thought-out ideas are!'

'Come on, it's better than you running up and down to London, isn't it?'

'I suppose so.'

It occurred to me that it was nice to have someone to talk to when I came in at the end of the day, but I pushed the thought firmly aside. I pointed a finger at George instead. 'But you're going to help! I hold you entirely responsible for the whole thing. If it wasn't for you, I could have got away with a couple of cocktails at a male stripper bar.'

George linked his hands behind his head and suppressed a smile. 'Would that have been more your thing?'

'Oh, all right, I'd have hated that too, but at least it would have been over quickly.' I hunched a shoulder. 'I'm dreading this house party already. I hate parties.'

'Really?'

'I never feel I belong,' I said, remembering those awful parties my father had made me go to. One awful party in particular. 'I don't seem to fit in anywhere. I never have. Life with Mum was worlds apart from the life I had in my father's house, and after a while I didn't belong in either of them. It's always been like that,' I said.

I didn't expect George to understand. He was the guy at the centre of any party, the one everyone revolved around, the one who made the party start just by walking in the door.

'Saffron's friends all think I'm weird,' I added glumly. 'We've got absolutely nothing to say to each other. Still.' I put my hands on my thighs and made an effort to rouse myself. 'It's only one weekend and it's what Saffron wants. I just need to make a plan.'

'Well, I don't mind helping you with that,' said George. 'Let's do it in the pub.'

'I don't know...'

'Oh, come on, it's the least I can do to make up for land-ing you with a party to organise in the first place,' he ca-joled. 'It's not like a date, in case you're still wondering if I'm going to turn into that weirdo you were so concerned about! Think of it as repayment for the tea.' He saw me hesitating. 'And it's a lovely evening.'

It was. The earlier clouds had cleared to leave a sky flushed with the promise of spring, and the air was soft and enticing. In spite of myself, I glanced longingly out of the window.

There was no use pretending that I wasn't tempted. 'All right.' I looked down at my black trousers and the taupe jacket I wore over a long-sleeved T shirt. 'Give me five minutes to change.'

When I went back into the kitchen, I was pulling a car-digan over a simple blue T-shirt, and George's brows lifted at the sight of the mint-green skirt that stopped just above my knees. He got to his feet, eyeing my legs with undis-guised appreciation.

'You look nice,' he said. 'I've never seen your legs be-fore.'

I tugged down my sleeves in a self-conscious gesture, and willed the stupid flush to fade from my cheeks. 'I al-ways wear trousers for work.'

'I can see why. It would be far too distracting for your colleagues, otherwise.'

'I shouldn't have to worry about what I'm wearing,' I said grouchily, mainly because I was ruffled by the way he was looking at me. It was only a skirt, for heaven's sake! 'Do you think the men I work with care about what *they* look like? But if I want to be taken seriously, I have to look professional at all times.'

'That explains all the severe suits.'

'And why I like to wear a skirt sometimes when I'm not working.'

'You wore trousers last night,' George pointed out.

After some discussion, it had been decided that Saffron would spend the rest of the day with Roly, while George and I went back to work. Roly had been all for Saffron staying the night at the Hall too, but I had vetoed that, afraid that if Saffron got too comfortable she would never leave. We had compromised with the four of us meeting for dinner at the Hall, where plans for the pre-wedding party had grown ever more elaborate before I managed to extract my sister and take her back to the cottage. I knew that one night on my sofa bed would be more than enough for her.

'Of course,' I told George, remembering the evening with a grimace. Torn between the need to keep my sister under control, to please Roly and—most difficult of all—to ignore the warm amusement in George's eyes, I hadn't enjoyed dinner much. 'If I'm with a client, it's even more important to look competent.'

George held the door open for me. 'I don't think Roly was thinking like a client last night.'

'No.' I locked the door and tucked the key into my purse. Not that there was much point in locking up when every Tom, Dick and George had a key, but it was hard to break London habits. I glanced up at George. 'He *does* know that Saffron's getting married, doesn't he?'

'It would be hard not to with all the talk of weddings last night.'

'It's just…he seems very smitten,' I said, chewing the corner of my bottom lip. 'Saffron's so pretty, and she can be delightful when she wants, but she's never had to think about anyone but herself. I wouldn't want him to get hurt.'

'Are you worried about Roly himself, or about your client being upset?'

'Both,' I said frankly.

'Well, don't. Roly's obviously besotted with your sister, but he'll be content to adore her from afar. He has surprisingly old-fashioned notions about being a gentleman, and he'd never take out any disappointment on you.'

I'd been surprised, in fact, that Saffron hadn't shown more interest in George, but she clearly didn't know quite what to make of him, and she didn't have the sharpest sense of humour in the world. Mind you, who needed a sense of humour when you had silver gilt hair, emerald eyes and a siren's body?

Saffron clearly felt much more at home with Roly's uncritical adoration. George had teased her and flattered her, but it was obvious that he wasn't bowled over by her.

I tried really hard not to feel pleased about that.

The Whellerby Arms was a traditional village pub. It had a low, beamed ceiling, plain, serviceable wooden furniture and was mercifully free of slot machines, piped music or padded banquettes.

I found a table in the corner while George went to the bar, and got out my notebook and pen. Gathering up the cardboard coasters and stacking them in a neat pile, I watched George under my lashes. There was a lot of laughing and back-slapping and hand-shaking going on. I saw him bend his head down to an elderly man who was leaning on the bar. He was listening intently, nodding, and then he smiled and a strange feeling stirred in the pit of my stomach.

Hunger, I told myself firmly. I hoped George would bring some nuts.

He did. I pounced on the packet as he tossed it onto the table and tore it open.

'No lunch,' I said through a mouthful of peanuts.

I had chosen to sit on the wooden trestle with my back to the wall, assuming that George would take the stool opposite. Too late, I remembered that it was a mistake to make assumptions as far as George was concerned, and to my dismay he sat beside me and stretched out his long legs.

He lifted his glass. 'Cheers.'

'Cheers,' I mumbled, edging surreptitiously away.

I really resented the way George made me nervous. I wasn't the type to lose my head over a handsome face. I'd done that once before, and I was never going to make that mistake again. I believed that integrity and humour and intelligence were far more attractive than looks, and yet the moment my gaze caught the lean line of his jaw or the creases around his eyes or that telltale dent in his cheek, which deepened when he was trying not to smile, my heart would stumble and a warmth would uncoil unnervingly inside me. It was all very unsettling.

To distract myself, I brushed the peanut crumbs from my fingers, pushed my hair behind my ears, and picked up my pen. 'SAFFRON'S PARTY,' I wrote neatly at the top of the page. '1. Invitations. 2. Costumes. 3. Caterers.'

'You're very organised,' said George.

'I'm going to manage this like any other project,' I said, pausing to pop a few more peanuts in my mouth. 'That means have a clear plan, and setting SMART goals.'

'Sounds efficient.' He lounged beside me, his solid thigh only inches from mine. 'What's a smart goal when it's at home?'

'Specific, Measurable, Attainable, Realistic and Time-bound.' I ticked them off on my fingers.

That dent in his cheek deepened. 'It's a party, Frith. There's only one goal for a party, and that's for everyone to have a good time.'

'That's all you know.' I clicked my teeth pityingly. 'This

party is about a lot more than that. It's about impressing all Saffron's friends and boosting her reputation. People only get to have a good time once that's achieved, and that means I'm going to have to do more than shove some white wine in a bucket of ice and put out a few bowls of crisps.

'That's where the goals come in,' I told him, tapping my pen against my list. 'You've got to be specific about what needs to be done. Take the dinner.' I had managed to talk Saffron out of a full-scale ball and we had agreed a formal dinner for a maximum of thirty guests in the state dining room. 'I can barely manage cheese on toast,' I admitted, 'so I'm going to have to find some local caterers who can produce a spectacular Edwardian banquet.'

'Why don't you ask Mrs Simms?' said George.

'I thought she was the housekeeper?'

'She is, but she's a brilliant cook too. She'd need some help, of course, but she's got various nieces in the village, and extra work is always welcome.'

'OK, that sounds good.' I drew a neat arrow next to 'Caterers' and wrote 'Contact Mrs Simms.' 'Excellent.' I tapped the pen thoughtfully against my teeth, then added 'Menu, Accommodation, Decoration, Games???' to my list before noticing that George wasn't paying attention. He was looking at my knees instead, and I wriggled a bit so that I could tug my skirt down.

'Do you run your whole life like this?' he asked, sounding distracted.

'All the time,' I said.

'What about relationships?'

'What about them?'

'You can't plan a relationship.'

'I disagree,' I said. 'I don't have time for a serious relationship in my current-five year plan, but that will definitely figure in my next one. I'll be thirty-three by then, and it might be time to think about settling down.'

George was staring at me. 'You're kidding? You actually have a five-year plan? Like a totalitarian regime?' He laughed. 'Do you give yourself quotas and send in the secret police if you don't make them?'

Colour crept up my throat. 'It's well established that clear goals are the key to a successful career,' I said stiffly.

'So what's your plan for finding that serious relationship?' George picked up his beer and eyed me over the rim of his glass. 'Do you have a smart goal for that too?'

He obviously thought I was nuts, but I didn't care. 'It's too early to be specific. I'm working on this five-year plan for now.'

'How does Whellerby fit into your plan?'

'Hugh was my mentor when I first joined the firm in London,' I said. 'He was really supportive, and I missed him when he left to set up his own design and build company up here, although I knew he wanted to come home to Yorkshire. His wife always stayed here, and he'd go down to London for the week, and I think he got fed up of the travelling.

'It was such a shame that he had the heart attack just when he'd got the big contract with the Whellerby estate. The conference centre will make his reputation locally, so it's just as important for us that it's a success and we stick to the budget as it is for you.'

'Hugh must think a lot of you if you're the one he asked to come and help him out,' George said.

I turned my own glass between my hands, thinking about how much I owed Hugh. 'He knew I wanted some site experience. I was just working on highway contracts in London, and my next step is to go overseas and work on a really major construction project. They're going to build a new airport in Shofrar, and if I could get on that, then I'd be in a good position to be promoted to senior engineer by the end of my five years.'

'I see.' George set down his beer. 'And then, once you're promoted, you're going to look around for a relationship?'

'Exactly. Another civil engineer makes sense. He'd understand about moving around from project to project, and we could go together if necessary. Plus, I only ever meet engineers.'

'I'm not an engineer,' said George. 'You've met me.'

'Only temporarily,' I said, a bit thrown. 'As soon as Hugh is better, I'm going to apply for a job in Shofrar. Besides,' I said, 'we've already established that you're not my type.'

'Only because you're a lookist.'

'Because I'm *sensible.*'

'But what about passion, Frith?' George shook his head. 'What about love? You can't reduce that to a plan.'

I'd tidied up the coasters, so George had put the glasses straight onto the table where they left wet rings. I moved my glass around, making a precise pattern.

'I'm not looking for love or passion,' I said. 'I've seen what happens when it goes. My mother gave up everything for my father. She could have had a career of her own, but she chose to help him set up his business instead. So when he got bored of us, she had nothing.'

'She had you.'

Very carefully, I completed my circle of ring marks and placed my glass in the middle. 'I wasn't enough,' I said.

It was the first time I had said that out loud. I had been good, and I had worked hard, and I had done everything she asked of me, and I had always felt guilty because I wasn't enough.

'Mum retrained. She took care of me. She did everything she could to make a good life for us together. She loved

me, I know,' I said, while part of me was marvelling that
I should be telling this to George Challoner of all people.
'But I don't think she ever got over my father. I don't think
she ever stopped loving him.'

I sighed. 'The truth is, she was never truly happy without
him. I'll never know, but I wonder if when that embolism
struck, there wasn't a moment that she was glad. Part of
my mother just gave up after my father left. Without him,
life didn't hold anything for her.'

'Tough on you,' said George.

'You can't plan for emotions,' I said. 'You can't predict
what people are going to do or feel, but you can think about
the practicalities of living and working and choose to make
a relationship with someone who understands those.'

'So you stick to engineers?'

I thought about my boyfriends, and it didn't take long.
It wasn't as if I'd had a whole string of relationships. Nick
had been a fellow engineering student, and we'd parted
ways amicably after we graduated. I'd worked with John
in London until he got a job overseas, and then there had
been Phil, but the truth was that neither of us were that
bothered, and I suspect it was a relief to us both when I
accepted Hugh's offer and went north.

It was an unimpressive record. Not that I had any intention of admitting that to George.

I nodded. 'It's more convenient to date engineers.'

'Convenient?' He shook his head. 'How many of these
convenient guys have made your heart beat faster, Frith?'

I avoided his eyes. And the question. 'I've been friends
with all of them.'

'And I'll bet you kept them all at arm's length,' said
George. 'You didn't let any of them jog you out of your
calm, ordered life, am I right?'

Of course he was right. I had deliberately played safe.

I'd only ever been out with men who were more friends than lovers, so when they left it wouldn't hurt at all. And to make sure, I had always ended things first.

'I don't *want* to be jogged out of it,' I said. 'I don't want to get into a state and not be able to concentrate on work because I'm waiting for the phone to ring. I don't want to spend my life fixating on one person and pinning all my happiness on him.'

'Poor Frith,' said George. 'Haven't you ever longed to throw caution to the wind and let yourself go, just for once?'

My mind flickered to Charles. Once, I had. It wasn't a mistake I would be making again.

'There are worse things than never having been in love,' I said.

'It just seems such a waste,' said George, studying my face with those disquieting blue eyes. 'You look so cool always, but then I look at your mouth, and I can't help feeling that there's all this passion bottled up inside you.'

'Oh, please,' I said, rolling my eyes.

'It's actually quite exciting,' he went on. 'You know, like one of those fantasies where a stern teacher suddenly whips off her specs, shakes out her hair and turns into a sexpot.'

'I have no intention of whipping or shaking anything,' I said, taking a prim sip from my glass. 'Besides, you're not one to talk,' I went on, anxious to move the conversation away from my non-existent sex life. 'I notice you're living on your own. How come you haven't taken the plunge into a passionate marriage if it's such a good idea?'

'I've tried,' said George and I paused with the glass halfway to the table.

'You're divorced?'

'No, we didn't get as far as the wedding. Annabel called it off when I got fired.'

'You were *fired*? What did you do? Or shouldn't I ask?'

'Not very much, that was part of the problem.' George picked up his glass and studied the beer as he swirled it around. 'Annabel made the right decision. I'm amazed that she ever agreed to marry me in the first place, to be honest. I was a mess in those days.'

I shifted on the settle so that I could look at him. I was surprised. George Challoner struck me as many things, but a mess wasn't one of them.

'You've changed.'

'I hope so,' he said. 'I'm not proud of what I was like then. I grew up in a wealthy family too,' he told me after a moment. 'Life was all mapped out. You'd have approved,' he added with a sidelong glance. 'The family had a plan. I was destined for the family bank, in spite of the fact that I had no qualifications and all I wanted to do was work with horses.'

Family bank? I sat up straighter. 'You're not one of *those* Challoners?'

'I am.' George's smile was twisted. 'Or, I was.'

Even I had heard of Challoners Bank, one of the most prestigious investment banks in London. Challoners had been bankers to the British establishment for generations, and were notoriously stuffy. None of Kevin Taylor's headline-grabbing antics for the Challoners. They moved in a different world from my father. They never flaunted their undoubted wealth, but no one doubted their power and influence. There were Challoners in politics and the law and on the boards of blue chip companies across the land.

And, apparently, in Whellerby.

No wonder he had that glossy assurance that had reminded me so bitterly of Charles when I'd first seen him.

'My parents take the family name very seriously,' George said. 'They don't believe in passion either. Their marriage was a business merger as far as I can tell, and

Harry and I investments for the future. We were shipped off to boarding school as soon as possible, and were supposed to move seamlessly on to Oxford, after which a nice little position would be found for us in the bank so that we could fast track to the board and continue the great Challoner tradition.'

I had never heard George sound bitter before. 'And you didn't oblige?'

'No. Harry knuckled down, but I was the family's black sheep right from the start. I was a pain in the arse, and my parents despaired of me, which was the point, obviously. Eventually I got myself expelled, and there was no question of Oxford after that.'

I was trying to imagine George as a rebel, but it was hard. He was so easy with people now, so annoyingly charming, that I just couldn't picture him being surly or difficult.

'There was a family conference, after which it was decided to ship me out of the country for a while. I had one of the best years of my life working on a ranch in Montana, but when they thought I had learnt my lesson I was summoned home.'

George pulled down his mouth as he set his glass on the table. 'If I'd had any guts, I'd have refused,' he said, 'but I took the easy option. An allowance, a car, a "job" in the bank…I could have said no to all of that, and lived my own life, but I didn't.'

'You were young,' I said. 'Everyone makes mistakes when they're young.'

'You didn't.'

'I was a good girl at school, but I've made plenty of other mistakes, believe me,' I said, thinking of Charles.

'I was old enough to know better,' said George, clearly determined to flay himself. 'I knew what I was doing, but instead of holding out for what I really wanted, I gave in. Nobody thought I was capable of much, so I was given a token directorship in human resources. I wasn't required to do much more than turn up occasionally and sign where was required.'

His jaw hardened. 'I didn't need to live down to my family's expectations of me, but I did. It was like I was determined to show them how useless I could really be. I threw myself into the party circuit. I was a walking, talking cliché for excess. But of course, I was a Challoner, so I could get away with it.'

'You can't have been that bad if you got engaged,' I said.

'Ah, Annabel…' His smile twisted. 'I really thought she could save me.'

'What was she like?'

'She was a country girl, or so I thought. Her family were into hunting, fishing and shooting, and she loved horses and dogs. She had some so-called PR job, but basically she was doing the social season, and looking for a husband. I thought she wanted what I wanted, a way out,' said George. 'I thought she was bored with the endless parties and pointless socialising.'

I don't know why, but I took against the idea of Annabel straight away.

'Nobody was forcing her to stay in London, were they?' I said sharply. 'If she'd wanted a way out, she could have got herself a job in the country and bought her own horse instead of waiting for a husband to do it for her!'

'The Annabels of this world don't think like you do, Frith. And nor did I then. I had this idealised notion of country living too. Harry and I used to go and stay with my grandmother during the holidays. She lived—still does—in a wonderful old manor house, full of dogs and cats, and she had a stable full of horses.

'My happiest times were spent there,' he said with a reminiscent smile. 'I wanted that again, and I still do, but I wasn't as brave as you. I didn't think of washing dishes to get what I wanted. I was lazy and useless and my family were right to fire me, because I certainly didn't know what I was doing at the bank, and I hated every moment I was there.'

'So I'm guessing Annabel decided you weren't such a good bet as a husband once you didn't have the Challoner fortune behind you?'

'Something like that,' said George ruefully. 'I shouldn't have been surprised, but I was. I thought she was so sweet and she was ready to settle down, but...well, anyway,' he finished with a shrug.

I took the pile of coasters and placed them in a straight line. 'Let me guess, she was a good cook?'

'Yes, she was.'

'And pretty, I presume?'

'Ravishing.' He slid me another glance as I arranged the coasters into a square. 'And she was fun—and sexy as hell.'

'Oh, please, not the old sweet-sexy-fun cliché,' I pretended to yawn, and was pleased to see the smile tugging at the corners of his mouth.

'It was boring of me, wasn't it?'

'Very,' I said. 'Next time, fall in love with someone more interesting.'

Then I made the mistake of looking into his eyes. I'd meant it as a joke, but I found myself trapped, pinioned by their blueness and their laughter and something else that drove the breath from my lungs and set my pulse thudding.

'Maybe I will,' he said.

There was a small, perilous silence.

He was teasing. He was *teasing*, I told myself feverishly, but it didn't stop me feeling as if I had just missed a step in the dark. My heart was stumbling clumsily around in my chest, getting in the way of the air I was still trying to suck back into my lungs.

Somehow I managed to drag my gaze away. 'Well, it shouldn't be too hard for you to find a girl who likes to cook and rides horses,' I said. 'Whellerby must be chock-a-block with women like that.'

'Yes, but I want to find the right one, and it's not that easy,' said George, just as his stupid phone started ringing. I say ringing, but it was that ridiculous squawk, mercifully muffled by his trouser pocket.

PICK UP THE PHONE! PICK UP THE PHONE! HEY YOU, YES YOU, IT'S YOUR PHONE RINGING! PICK UP THE PHONE!

I rolled my eyes. 'Don't mind me,' I said as George fished the phone out of his pocket and checked the caller.

'No, it's OK. I'll call back later.'

Of course, I immediately wondered who had been calling. Someone fresh-faced and pretty in jodhpurs with a pinny around their waist, I decided sourly. George was probably working his way through all the suitable candidates.

'Where were we?' said George.

'You were finding it hard to find a domestic goddess.'

'Oh, yes. Perhaps I should try your SMART goals. I'm very specific about what I want, so in theory I ought to be able to find someone who ticks all the boxes.'

'You'd have to ask her if she was prepared to put up with that stupid ringtone!'

George tutted. 'The trouble with you, Frith, is that you've no sense of fun. I'll bet you've got a really boring ringtone.'

'There's nothing wrong with my phone.'

'What's your number?' he demanded. 'I'm going to ring it.'

Sure enough, a discreet buzz from my phone announced that I had a call.

'That's pathetic,' said George. 'That's the sort of ring-tone that belongs to a woman who wears sensible white cotton underwear and has no idea how to have a good time.'

I put up my chin. 'I'm perfectly capable of having a good time,' I said, avoiding the question of my underwear, which did indeed verge on the sensible side. First day off I had, I was going to buy myself something red and lacy, I decided, before catching myself up. I absolutely did not care what George thought of my underwear. Not that he would ever see it.

Now I was getting flustered. I reached for my purse to disguise the pinkness in my cheeks. 'In fact, I'm so ready to have a good time I'll go and get another round.'

'Hold on,' said George, holding up a hand. 'Have you formulated a proper plan?' he asked in mock concern. 'I don't think you should rush into this. What's your strategy for getting to the bar? Is your goal a SMART one?'

I stuck out my tongue as I wriggled past him. 'Do you want another pint or not?'

The bar was crowded and it was a while before I was able to push my way through to the front to be served. When I got back to the table, George was looking innocent.

'What?' I said suspiciously.

He spread his hands. 'Nothing.'

'Hmmph.' A group on the neighbouring table had filched our stool, so I had no choice but to squeeze back onto the settle with George.

'Here's to reaching our goals,' I said, touching my glass to George's.

'To goals,' he agreed. 'And fun.'

CHAPTER FOUR

THE moment I saw George…!

I was in a towering rage when I left work the next day. I slammed Audrey's door so hard, she shuddered, but, clearly recognising that I was in no mood for messing, started immediately.

Planning the most horrible forms of revenge I could think of, I drove back to the cottage, only to slam on the brakes when I saw the cause of my fury riding across a field. He seemed to be heading towards the gate, so I pulled Audrey up onto the verge. Closing the door with another slam to make her wince, I waited with my arms folded and a black look on my face.

Catching sight of me, George lifted a hand and urged the horse into a canter. Even at a distance his smile lit up the grey day and my treacherous pulse jumped, but that only made my scowl darken further. George wouldn't be smiling by the time I'd finished with him, I vowed.

I confess to some alarm as he got closer and I realised the size of the horse thundering towards me. For a terrifying moment I thought it was going to come crashing right through gate into me, and I quailed, but at the last second George pulled it up in a spray of mud, with a lot of snorting and thudding of hooves.

My heart was pounding so hard that I couldn't speak.

The horse was a great black thing with wild eyes and flaring nostrils. Its muscles bunched alarmingly as it sidled restlessly, tossing its head up and down, while George sat on its back as calmly as if on an armchair, his strong hands steady on the reins.

'Frith,' he greeted me. 'How's the hangover?'

Not that good, in fact, which hadn't improved my mood. I wasn't used to drinking, and I had stayed for a third round with George the night before. He had told me scurrilous and probably apocryphal stories about the locals and made me laugh, and then he had walked me home and said goodnight and hadn't tried to kiss me.

Which I was very relieved about, naturally.

In spite of the hangover and a vaguely disgruntled feeling, I had been feeling quite well disposed towards George. Until that phone call.

'I've got a bone to pick with you,' I said furiously, ignoring his question.

'What have I done?' he asked with injured innocence.

'You know very well what, you…you…you…!' I shook my finger up at him, stuttering as I searched for a bad enough word.

'Careful!' George covered the horse's ears with his hands in mock consternation. 'You mustn't shock Jasper. He's very sensitive.'

'Everything's a big joke to you, isn't it?' I said bitterly.

George swung himself off the horse in one fluid motion and looped the reins over its head so that he could come and lean on the other side of the gate.

'You look very cross,' he said. 'Like a ruffled robin.'

'I'm a lot more than cross! I'm furious! I'm incandescent!'

I was glad not to have to crane my neck to look up at him on the horse, but, on the other hand, I wished he hadn't brought it with him to the gate. At close quarters, Jasper was *enormous*.

I was determined not to show that I was nervous—*Annabel* wouldn't have been nervous, I told myself—but I kept a wary eye on the head hanging over the gate.

'I'm so angry I—' I ranted on, but Jasper chose that moment to lunge towards me with his great yellow teeth and I jumped back with a squeak of alarm and lost my thread.

'Right,' said George. 'Call me oversensitive, but I'm getting the definite feeling that you're in a bad mood.'

I sucked in a breath and set my teeth. 'I was in a meeting—an *important* meeting—with the environmental consultants this morning when my phone rang,' I said, rigidly controlled now. 'Of course, I didn't realise it was my phone at first, because I didn't recognise the ringtone, did I? Because *somebody* had changed it!

'Do you have *any* idea how embarrassing it was to be standing there with all those men listening to some sultry woman announcing that she was too sexy for her shirt?' I demanded.

George laughed.

'I'm glad you think it's funny,' I went on between gritted teeth. 'Because nobody else did. We all just stood there while this breathy voice went on and on about being too sexy. Nobody knew where to look!'

To my fury, the corner of his mouth twitched.

'It took ages before I realised that it was my phone!' I remembered, mortified. 'I looked an absolute idiot, and it was all your fault!' I shoved the phone at him. 'I know you did it when I was getting the drinks last night, so you'd better change the ringtone back to normal *right now,* or I won't be answerable for the consequences!'

'Frith Taylor, are you telling me you don't know how to change your own ringtone?'

'I tried. I just made it louder,' I said grittily. 'You messed it up, you put it right.'

George sighed but took the phone and squinted down at it as he began pressing random buttons, apparently unconcerned by the enormous bulk of the horse dancing around beside him.

'I have to work so hard to get these men to take me seriously,' I went on, watching him fretfully, 'and you come along and ruin it!'

'You need to lighten up, Frith.' He handed the phone back to me. 'Those guys were probably intimidated by you before, but now they know that you're human after all and have a sense of humour, I bet you'll get on better.'

'Well, thanks for the career advice,' I said sarcastically, 'but I think I'd prefer a grovelling apology.'

'How about I take you for another drink instead?'

'No, thank you,' I said coldly. I stalked back to Audrey, my dignified exit ruined by treading in a cow pat. 'I shall be staying in tonight—alone!'

I sat behind my desk in the site office, glowering out at the rain that drummed on the cabin's flat metal roof and obscured my view of the foundations, where work had been abandoned earlier.

I was not in a good mood. Again. And it was George's fault. Again.

I hadn't been able to sleep, and spent most of the night pummelling my pillow and kicking the duvet off and on, and off again. When I did eventually drop off, I dreamt of George, controlling the huge horse with calm hands. I was there too, but on the wrong side of the gate. George swung off Jasper, as he'd done the evening before, but this time he let the reins go as he walked towards me. In the dream, I was very worried about the huge horse wandering around

free, but I couldn't move. I could just stand there with my
back to the gate while George reached out and started to
unbutton my shirt with deft fingers.

'Don't worry about Jasper,' he said as I squirmed with
anticipation. 'He doesn't bite.'

Then the horse was right there, shoving his great nose at
me, and I lurched awake, my heart pounding with a mixture of fright and frustration.

A black horse! It was such a clichéd symbol of sexual
frustration that I was embarrassed.

So George had nice hands and could control a horse. Big
deal. That didn't make up for him being the most annoy-
ing, irritating, infuriating man on the planet.

And now it was raining. No, not raining, *pouring*. There
was no way the men could do anything useful in this. With
a sigh, I adjusted the fierce glasses I wore for working at
the computer. If only you could fit the British weather into
a plan, life would be a lot easier.

A stamping of boots on the metal steps outside made me
look up, and the next moment George appeared in the doorway. He wore a battered waxed jacket and muddy boots,
and his hair was plastered to his head, and at the sight of
him, my senses crisped instantly. It was as if the air itself
jolted, and I was acutely aware of the drumming rain and
the soft whirr of my computer. Of the smooth cotton shirt
against my skin and my thighs pressing into my chair.

I thought about how he had smiled as he unbuttoned my
shirt in my dream, and my mouth dried.

'What are you doing here?' I demanded, snatching off
my glasses.

'Getting out of the rain.' George shook himself like a
dog, spraying raindrops everywhere, and I moved my papers ostentatiously.

'Hey!' I objected, although the water was pooling around George rather than my desk.

'Sorry,' he said, 'but it's a bit wet out there.'

'What's wrong with the estate office?'

'Really, Frith, anyone would think you weren't pleased to see me.' He took off his jacket and hung it up next to my hard hat.

'I can't imagine why you'd think that!' I said, the ring-tone incident still rankling, as he toed off his boots.

Padding across the office in his socks, George threw himself down in the chair on the other side of my desk. 'All right,' he said. 'I'm sorry. It was naughty of me, but I couldn't resist…and if that isn't a grovelling enough apology, I've brought you lunch to make amends. Judging by the way you hoovered up those peanuts the other night, you're not getting enough lunch.'

'I'm used to popping out for a sandwich in London,' I said. 'There's nowhere to pop out *to* here, even if it did stop raining long enough to go out.'

'Here go you. Try this.' He tossed one of the packets across the desk to me.

'What is it?'

'One of Mrs Simms's ham and mustard sandwiches,' he told me, settling more comfortably into his chair. 'They're the best.'

I opened the sandwich. I had to admit it looked good. Home-made bread, thick butter, properly carved ham and a good smear of mustard.

'I suppose I *could* have some lunch,' I said. 'It's not as if there's anything else to do when the weather's like this.'

More eyebrow waggling from George. 'Oh, I don't know, I'm sure we could think of something.'

Before I could think of a suitably crushing reply, there

was a knock on the side of the cabin and Frank put his head round the door.

'There's no sign of it clearing up,' he told me and I sighed.

'No. You might as well go, Frank.'

George had swung round in his chair. 'I see you're skiving off as usual, Frank,' he said with a grin.

'Only on the boss's say-so,' said Frank, nodding at me. 'She might just be a slip of a lass, but she knows what she's about.'

'Is that right?' George's blue eyes rested speculatively on my face, and I put my glasses back on to hide my beastly blush.

'Yes, well…see you tomorrow, Frank.'

'Righty-oh.' Frank turned to go and then paused. 'You won't forget that ringtone for Dave, will you? He's that chuffed about it.'

'Er…no, of course not,' I began just as George lifted an eyebrow.

'Ringtone?'

Frank actually chuckled. 'Get the boss here to give you a listen to her ringtone sometime. It gave us all a good laugh this morning, I can tell you! We'd heard from the lads at the council that she'd taken them all by surprise yesterday—apparently they were all in hysterics after the meeting—but this one was even better. Now Dave wants to get the same one for his Betty's birthday. We all like a lass with a sense of humour.'

There was a silence in the office as he left with a friendly nod to us both. We listened to his boots clumping down the steps, followed by the slam of a car door.

George looked at me.

'Oh, very well, you might as well say it!' I said crossly and he laughed.

'I told you they'd like it,' he said.

'OK, they thought the ringtone was funny,' I admitted, 'but you had no business changing it to something equally silly,' I told him, remembering my horror that morning when the phone had first rung. 'You knew perfectly well I wanted you to put my normal ringtone back!'

'I couldn't resist,' he said, holding up his hands in surrender at my fierce look.

'Now I've got to tell them all where to get hold of a ringtone that quacks and chortles.'

I pushed my glasses up onto my forehead so I could knuckle under my tired eyes. 'I suppose I should be grateful you picked that and not the orgasm scene from *When Harry Met Sally* or something equally embarrassing—and don't even *think* about it!' I warned as George's face lit up. 'I'll admit that your little stunt has improved my relationship with the guys on site—and my reputation in the council offices, apparently!—but no more, all right?'

George crossed his fingers and held them up. 'Scout's honour,' he mumbled through a mouthful of sandwich.

I might as well accept the inevitable. I pushed back my chair. 'Want some coffee?' I asked and he stuck up a thumb.

I made the coffee and plonked his mug in front of him before taking mine round to my own seat. It felt easier with the desk between us.

It was a delicious sandwich, I had to admit, and my enjoyment was spoiled only by the fact that when George had finished his, he tipped back in his chair at a dangerous angle so that he could put his feet up on my desk.

'Do you mind?' I said pointedly.

'What's the problem?'

'Your dirty socks are the problem! Could you please take them off my desk and stop tilting that chair like that? It's making me nervous. I don't care if you break your neck, but I've got a health and safety record to think about.'

George sighed and swung his feet down. 'It seems to me health and safety regulations were invented just to stop the rest of us having fun.'

'It's perfectly possible to have fun without risking injury,' I said primly, and then wished I hadn't because George leant forward and waggled his eyebrows at me suggestively.

'How do you have fun, Frith? Do you have a five-year plan for that too?'

I pressed my lips together and glared at him, almost glad when my mobile went off and spared me the need to reply.

I use the words 'went off' advisedly. I leapt in my seat as a maniacal cackling and quacking filled the room. 'You're not leaving here until you've changed this,' I said to George, who was grinning, idiot that he was.

Snatching up the phone, I answered it just to shut up the noise. 'Hello,' I snapped.

'Frith, it's me.'

'Oh…Saffron.'

Please God, let it not be another forty-five minutes on whether the guests would think three thousand pounds a bottle too mean, which pair of Jimmy Choos would go best with Saffron's dress, or the exact shade of the specially woven silk coverings for the chairs.

Evidently prepared for a long wait, George tipped back in his chair and put his feet back on the desk.

'I'm doing the seating plan,' moaned Saffron. 'It's *so* difficult.'

'It must be,' I said, not really listening. I pointed at George's feet and mouthed *Down!*

Needless to say, he just smiled blandly back at me. It wasn't a challenge I was about to resist. Saffron wittered on in my ear as I went round and tried to lift George's legs onto the floor. I was hampered by the fact that one hand was holding the phone, but even so he was incredibly strong.

Refusing to give up, I wrestled one-armed with his legs while he just leant back in his chair and smiled at my puny efforts. It was only when I could feel my face turning red with effort that I realised how absurd I was being, and I started to giggle silently. George was smothering his own laughter and in the end I had to press the phone against my shoulder so that Saffron wouldn't realise just how little attention she was getting.

'You can see what a problem it is,' Saffron was saying as I admitted defeat and perched on the edge of the desk next to George's feet while I recovered.

'Absolutely.'

'So I'll sort out a date for you, then?'

Any lingering desire to giggle vanished as the smile was wiped off my face. 'What?' I said, startled. 'What for?'

'I've just been *explaining*!' Saffron heaved a martyred sigh. 'A singleton looks so odd on the top table. I could ask Daddy not to bring his new girlfriend, but she's such an attention seeker, she'd probably make a fuss. Anyone would think she was the only supermodel on the planet!'

It was the first I had heard about my father's latest girlfriend. He had never remarried after Saffron's mother had left, but was careful to be seen with a string of spectacular beauties, none of whom had gone down well with Saffron. If there was any attention-seeking going on, Saffron liked to be the one who was doing it, and she had no time for any attempts to outshine her.

I guessed that a supermodel sitting next to you on the top table wasn't any bride's dream but if Saffron loved anyone, it was her adoring father, and if he wanted his girlfriend there, Saffron would put up with it for his sake.

'Of course, if I explained about the odd numbers, I'm sure he'd understand,' said Saffron hopefully.

Tell my father that he would have to leave his gorgeous girlfriend behind so that he could sit next to his ugly duckling daughter, too boring to be able to get a boyfriend of her own? I didn't *think* so.

'Don't involve Dad,' I told Saffron quickly.

'I'll ask Piers, then. His girlfriend will be on a shoot at the wedding, and I'm sure he wouldn't mind being your date for the wedding.'

Without wanting to, I found myself looking at George, who could obviously hear every word. He smirked at me and gave me the thumbs up.

I smiled back at him, sweetly. 'Don't worry about a date for me,' I told Saffron without stopping to let myself think. 'I'm bringing my boyfriend.'

'You've got a boyfriend?' Saffron sounded surprised, as well she might.

'Didn't I tell you?' I said. 'It's George.'

George's chair tipped forward abruptly, and his feet crashed to the floor.

Result.

'George?' Saffron echoed blankly.

'You remember him when you were up here? Roly's friend?'

'Oh, yes.' I could practically see Saffron's expression clearing. 'I didn't know you two were...you know.' For such a sophisticated socialite, Saffron could be surprisingly prudish. 'Why didn't you tell me?'

'I haven't told anyone else,' I said, wriggling my bottom more comfortably on the desk and getting into my story. I was beginning to enjoy myself. 'To be honest, Saffron, this is just a physical thing for me. George is absolutely mad about me, but you know what I'm like. I hate being crowded. It makes things awkward on the site when he's hanging around like a lovesick puppy.'

Lovesick puppy? George mouthed in disgust and I spread my hands in a what-can-you-do? gesture.

'I haven't told George this yet,' I confided in Saffron, 'but I'm just having a good time with him until I go overseas. He's got a good body, and I'm not interested in anything else. I mean, it's nice to be adored, don't get me wrong, but I can see me getting bored with him pretty quickly. Still, it's something to do in the evenings up here and he'll brush up OK for the wedding, so put him down as my date.'

'Well, all right, but I wish you'd told me before,' said Saffron with a huffy little sigh. 'It would have saved me a lot of worry about the seating plan.'

'You don't need to panic,' I told George when I finally managed to get Saffron off the phone.

'You're the one who should be panicking,' he said, amused. 'Now you've got to take me to the wedding and persuade me to act like a lovesick puppy!'

'OK, I'm sorry about that, but it served you right for messing around with my ringtones,' I said. I was back in my chair, turning the phone round and round in my hands as the implications of what I had just done began to sink in. 'And you won't really have to go, of course. I'll make some excuse to Saffron.'

'You can't make it my fault,' said George. 'Remember how mad I am about you!'

'I'll tell her I'm getting bored with you.' I pursed my lips as I thought. 'I'll drop a few hints about your performance in bed, which is frankly a little…disappointing, shall we say? It's going to turn out that you're really not man enough to satisfy me. Saffron will understand.'

George's eyes glinted appreciatively. 'I'm not sure she will. Having met your sister, I'd have thought she'd need a lot more than a lousy lover as a reason for throwing out her seating plan.'

Unfortunately, all too true.

Perhaps I *had* got a little carried away, I thought. I would have to ring Saffron straight back and explain that I had been joking. Which might take some time. Saffron's wedding was a Very Serious Business and she wouldn't take kindly to the idea of me making light of it.

My heart sank at the prospect of the conversation.

'I'll ring her tomorrow,' I said. 'There's still time for her to fix me up with this Piers person. Apparently he's prepared to take me on as a pity date,' I added glumly.

'It won't be much of a pity date if Saffron tells him how you've been using me as your sex toy.'

'Oh, she won't tell him that.' I pulled down the corners of my mouth. 'I can hear her already: "Frith's quite old and she's a bit eccentric. She actually has a career—no, I don't know how to spell that either, it's too shaming—but if you could bear to be seen with her, Piers darling, I'll make sure you get in on the photos in *Glitz*…"' I sighed. 'It's pretty humiliating when your date has to be bribed to be seen with you.'

'I don't think you should go with anyone who needs to be bribed to be your date,' said George firmly.

'It's better than being paired off with my father,' I said, 'and the alternative is to be marooned on the top table with a big sign over my head saying "sad older sister on the shelf". Piers might not be a prince, but he'll be better than telling Saffron I'm going to mess up her seating plan completely,' I went on. 'I know she's a bit bridezilla at the moment, but this wedding is so important to her. I can put up with a bit of humiliation for a day.'

'Or you could take me, the way you told her,' said George.

'That was a joke!'

'Of course it was, but it's not a bad idea. Why *not* take me?'

I looked at him in astonishment. 'I couldn't ask you to do something like that!'

'Why not?'

'The wedding's going to be ghastly. You don't know the meaning of ostentation until you've seen Saffron's wedding plans! My father's spending over a million pounds on this wedding.' I grimaced with distaste. 'I love my sister, but talk about over the top…!'

George spread his hands. 'It won't bother me. I can have a good time anywhere.'

I stopped in the middle of a laugh. 'You're not serious?' I asked.

'I don't mind,' he said. 'I brush up OK, and I won't pick my nose in public or eat my peas off my knife.'

I could believe it. He had the assurance that would take him anywhere. George wouldn't be intimidated by the glossy celebrities or the flashing cameras the way I was.

I studied him across the desk. He had tipped his chair back in precisely the position he knew drove me mad and was looking back at me, his eyes blue, his brows raised humorously, the lopsided curl to his mouth creasing one cheek in a way that made me feel hollow inside. He was gorgeous, there was no other word for it.

Infuriating, unsettling, provoking but, yes, gorgeous.

I had no illusions about myself. I wasn't plain, but I was no beauty either. Unlike my lovely sister, I was just ordinary. Ordinary, practical and—it had to be faced—more than a little uptight. Not the kind of girl gorgeous men wanted to spend the weekend with.

As I remembered all too well. Charles had made that more than clear.

'Why would you want to do that?' I asked, and he smiled at the suspicion in my voice.

'I don't want you trashing my reputation as a red-hot lover.'

I just looked at him.

'All right,' he said, letting the front legs of his chair fall back to the floor as if to underline that he was serious. 'I've got to admit that it did occur to me when you were winding up your sister that we might be able to help each other. There's something you could do for me in return, if you felt like it.'

'There is?'

'Remember I told you about the grandmother Harry and I used to spend our holidays with?'

'The one with the horses and the dogs?'

'That's right.' George hesitated. 'She's ninety in June, and there's going to be a small family party at her house. When I spoke to her last night, she said she wanted me to be there.'

I could imagine how difficult that would be for him. I knew how I felt about having to see my father again at Saffron's wedding.

'Are you going to go?'

'I have to,' he said. 'Letitia's house was the only place that ever felt like home. She was wonderful to me and Harry. We loved being there. She gave me my first pony and taught me how to ride. If she wants me at her party, then I'll be there, but it's not going to be an easy occasion. I don't know if my parents and Harry even know she's invited me.'

'I can see why you wouldn't look forward to it,' I said, wondering just how badly he had messed up to be ostracised by his parents and his brother. He must have done something awful if they couldn't forgive him. 'But what's your grandmother got to do with me?'

For the first time since I'd met him, George seemed unsure. He got up and wandered over to the window where the rain was still pelting down.

'I was just thinking that it would make her really happy if I turned up with you.'

I stared at him in astonishment. 'With *me*?'

'Letitia would like you,' said George. 'She was always very dismissive of girlfriends I took there in the past. She said they were all "flibbertigibbets", and, to be fair to her, most of them were. I thought she'd approve of Annabel, but when I told her that the engagement was off she just sniffed and said I was well out of it. She said Annabel had no spine.'

'And you think I do?'

'Nobody looking at that straight back of yours could doubt it.' The warm blue eyes rested on me, and under his gaze I felt that dangerous curl of warmth flickering to life again inside me. Maybe having a spine wasn't as exciting as being sweet and sexy and fun, but, still, it was a compliment.

'It was Letitia who told me to stop messing around,' George went on. 'She said then that all she wanted was to see me settle down with a woman of integrity. "Find yourself a sensible girl," she told me, "and I can die happy." I've been trying to think about what I could take her as a present, and I honestly think that what she would like most was to believe that I had found the right woman.

'A woman like you, Frith,' he said, looking straight at me.

Sensible. I was. I kept my life firmly under control and you couldn't get more sensible than that, and yet I was unaccountably put out. I didn't mind having a spine, but *sensible*? Why not just come right out and call me dull?

'Of course, she doesn't have to know that you're the kind of girl who invents dates to foil her sister's seating plans,' said George, who had a truly unnerving ability to read my mind at times.

'You're not suggesting we get married and settle down just to keep your grandmother happy, I hope?' I said, more tartly than I intended.

'I wasn't thinking of going that far,' said George. 'It would be enough if she believed that I had met someone suitable and was thinking about it.'

'Are you sure you want to lie to your grandmother?'

'We don't need to pretend to be engaged or anything. That really would be a lie,' he agreed. 'But I *have* met you. That's not a lie. I think she'd like the idea that I had found someone she approved of.

'The family split has been hard on Letitia,' he went on when I said nothing. 'I'd like to make her feel as if everything was coming together and that she doesn't need to worry about me any more. Would that be so wrong?'

CHAPTER FIVE

I WENT to smooth my hair behind my ears and found it was already there. 'Pretending to be a couple feels like a lie,' I said. 'I'm not sure how comfortable I'd be deceiving your grandmother.'

'But you're comfortable deceiving your sister?'

'That feels different somehow. Saffron doesn't really care if you and I are really a couple. She only cares about her seating plan.'

'And you'd be taking me along because you care about *her*,' said George, leaning back against the photocopier and folding his arms. 'Sure, you can insist on being completely truthful. You could tell her that you're proud of your independence, that you're happy to go to her wedding on your own, and to hell with her seating plan, but you won't, will you?'

My eyes slid away from his. I wouldn't, and he knew it.

'I could tell Letitia that my future was none of her business and that I'd rather stick pins in my eyes than go and play happy families with my parents, but that would hurt her, and I don't want to do that, any more than you want to hurt Saffron.

'So yes,' he said, 'it would be a pretence, and it would be a kind of lying, but would it be so terrible?'

He straightened from the photocopier before I had a chance to answer.

'Why don't you think about it?' he said. 'But don't feel under any pressure. If you don't want to come to our happy family reunion, I certainly wouldn't blame you!' He was putting on his boots, reaching for his jacket. 'I'm happy to pretend to be your boyfriend at Saffron's wedding anyway,' he promised. 'I'm not going to turn down the chance to be with a sex kitten like you!'

Sex kitten. It was the first time I'd ever been called one of those! I tried to imagine what it would be like if George weren't joking, if he really did want to be with me because he couldn't keep his hands off me, and was embarrassed to find that a disquieting thrill snaked down my spine at the idea. Sensible I might be, but I still rather liked the thought of being too hot to handle, although I knew I'd never in a million years be able to pull it off.

'I prefer to think of myself as a tiger rather than a kitten,' I said with dignity, just in case he was afraid I was taking him seriously. I bared my teeth at him to make the point. 'Grrr.'

George grinned as he reached for the door, and I nearly forgot my sandwich. 'Thank you for lunch,' I said before he could close it behind him.

'You're welcome.' He put his head back round the door. 'Let me know what you decide.'

Would it be so terrible? I thought about George's question all that night.

It wasn't as if either of us had a partner who would be upset by the pretence. Quite the opposite, in fact, at least in my case. There was no use pretending that Saffron's wedding wouldn't be a lot more fun with George at my side.

I was proud of my independence, just as he had said, but

in the small hours I couldn't deny the fact that I hadn't been looking forward to being the lone singleton at Saffron's wedding. All Saffron's friends thought I was weird enough as it was. The thought of their faces when I turned up with a man like George on my arm was pleasing, it had to be admitted.

And it wasn't just her friends. The world and his wife had been invited to the wedding as far as I could make out. Exclusive rights to the photos had been sold to *Glitz*, the celebrity magazine. Did I really want to be identified as Saffron Taylor's lonely sister?

George had said that he would come to the wedding anyway, but fair was fair. He was right. What harm could it do to keep an old lady happy? I was thinking about George, too, much as it went against the grain. Whatever he had done to alienate his family, it wasn't going to be easy for him to face them again.

He wouldn't ask for it outright, but it seemed to me he could do with some support. I was twitchy enough about facing my father, and that would be at a wedding where there would be plenty of other people around to defuse the tension. There would be no avoiding George's parents and brother at his grandmother's party. I suspected George would feel very alone if he went on his own.

I don't know why it was that thought that made up my mind more than any other, but it did.

I wanted to tell George that I had made a decision before I lost my nerve. When I rang him, he said he was at the stables, so I drove over there when the men broke for lunch. I parked Audrey outside the handsome stable block, and went under an arch into the yard. Jasper had his handsome head over a stable door. He rolled his eyes at me as I gave him a wide berth, remembering my dream.

I found George in a stable where he was brushing down a chestnut mare. The horse stared at me curiously, and George straightened with a smile.

'Come and say hello to Mabel.'

'Er, hello, Mabel,' I said from the door, breathing in the distinctive smell of straw and horse.

George raised a brow. 'You're not frightened of horses, are you, Frith?'

'No...at least... They're very *big*, aren't they? I like to admire them from a distance.'

'Can you believe her?' George told the horse, who whickered and blew softly in his ear. 'Frith's afraid of a big softy like you.'

No doubt Annabel would have been skipping over to the horse without a moment's hesitation.

I put up my chin. 'I'm not afraid.'

'Then come closer.'

When I hesitated, he scratched Mabel's jaw, and the horse responded by nuzzling into him and blowing down his neck.

'Mabel used to be nervous too,' he said. 'When I first saw her she was in a terrible state. She'd been so badly treated, she would lash out if anyone came near her, but she learnt how to trust. If she can, you can.'

Well, I wasn't going to be outdone by a horse, especially not one that was *flirting* with him. There was no other word for it.

I marched across the stable, whipped out my hand, touched her nose and snatched my hand back to tuck it safely under my armpit.

Mabel looked puzzled.

'No, I don't call that a stroke either, Mabel,' said George. 'Come here,' he added to me.

'Really, I—'

I broke off with a gasp as George took hold of my waist and swung me into the shelter of his body, trapping me between him and Mabel's huge yellow teeth.

There was no choice. Flustered, I pressed back against him, excruciatingly aware of the solid length of George behind me.

'That's better,' he said. Keeping one arm around my waist, he tugged one of my hands out from the safety of my armpit and spread my fingers wide. Then, very slowly, he drew my palm down Mabel's nose. I was so close that I could see ridiculously long lashes over her liquid brown eyes. Her coat was stiff but smooth at the same time, and there were little grey hairs flecked between her eyes and towards the end of her nose where her nostrils flared.

She had long whiskers over velvety lips, and when I felt her warm breath on my palm, I felt something shift inside me.

'There, that wasn't so bad, was it?' George's voice in my ear made me remember that I was still held cosily within the circle of his arms, and I made myself step away.

My back was tingling where I had been pressed against him, and I didn't know what to do with my hands all at once. I tried them in various positions before settling on hugging my arms together.

I cleared my throat. 'Is she yours?'

'Mabel prefers to think that I'm hers,' said George. 'Letitia gave us to each other when I was sixteen. The best present I ever had,' he remembered, his voice warm with affection. 'That was nearly sixteen years ago, so she's an old lady now.'

'You said she was mistreated.' Looking at the sleek coat and trusting eyes, it was hard to believe. 'How could anyone do that?'

'I don't know, Frith. Luckily, they found her in time

and brought her to Letitia. My grandmother's an amazing
woman. She's got a magic touch for horses. They used to
call her the Wiltshire Whisperer locally, and any horse with
a behavioural problem would find its way to her eventually.
The local vets knew what she could do, and they were the
ones who brought Mabel in.'

He tugged affectionately at Mabel's wiry fringe, but his
face darkened at the memory. 'She'd been rescued from
the most appalling conditions, and she was so skittish, it
took a week before she'd let me close enough to touch her.'

'Poor thing.' I tried to imagine the horse butting her
nose so trustingly against George as traumatised but it was
hard to do.

'I was there with Letitia when they brought her in,'
George went on. 'I don't really remember why. I'd probably been chucked out of school. That happened at fairly
regular intervals. I've got a feeling I was angry about something, anyway. But as soon as I saw Mabel, I knew she
was special.'

He shook his head, unable to explain. 'I don't know why,
but there was a kind of connection between us, and when
Letitia saw that she let me work with Mabel all summer. I
spent hours and hours with her.'

'You must have had to be very patient,' I said. To be honest, I was having trouble picturing it. To me, George always
seemed to make the air around him snap and crackle with
energy and I couldn't see him as a steady sixteen-year-old.

'It took a long time, but winning Mabel's trust was the
best thing I ever did,' said George. He was gathering up
bits of tack and hanging them over the stall. 'At the end of
the summer, my grandmother said that I could keep her,
but of course there was no way I could take her to London,
so she stayed in Wiltshire and I rode her whenever I went
down to see Letitia.

'She's still in the same house—says she's going to be carried out in a box—but even she had to admit that the horses had got too much for her to manage a couple of years ago. She sold all of them, except Mabel, of course. Luckily, Roly had these stables, so I could bring her north with me.'

'I saw lots of other horses in the stables,' I said. 'Are they yours too?'

'Nope, Mabel's all I've got in the world,' said George, giving her a final affectionate slap on the rump and following me out into the yard. 'Some were old Lord Whellerby's hunters,' he said, shutting Mabel's door behind him. 'We've got a couple of retired racehorses too, and some that are recuperating after accidents or illnesses.'

He stopped to pat the neck of a bay who had its nose over its door and was flickering its ears. 'Toby here was hit by a car last year, and now he's too nervous to be ridden. I'm working with him to get over the trauma, but it's a slow process.'

'How did his owners know to bring him here?' I asked curiously and George shrugged.

'Word gets around. I'd really like to expand the stables so I can work with horses with other behavioural problems,' he said. 'There's so much I could do if we had more space and if—' He stopped with a self-conscious laugh. 'Well, they're just ideas.'

'It sounds like you've got a plan too,' I teased him.

'A very long-term one. There are lots of other things to do on the estate first, and Roly doesn't ride so the stables aren't a priority for him. I'm just taking on a few horses at the moment in my spare time.'

He looked at his watch. 'Have you had lunch?'

'No, but—'

'You can share my sandwich,' he said. 'I'll just go and wash my hands.'

'You can't keep feeding me,' I protested weakly when he reappeared with a foil packet and we settled ourselves on the stable block.

'Mrs Simms feeds me,' said George, 'so I'm just passing it on. I'll ask her to make an extra sandwich next week.'

'Oh, you can't do that!'

'She'd love to. Nothing makes her happier than feeding everyone up.' George unwrapped the foil and looked inside. 'Cheese and salad OK with you?'

'Lovely,' I said, succumbing to temptation. I was hungry.

He took out half of the sandwich and passed the foil to me. 'Have you asked Mrs Simms about Saffron's party yet?'

'No, I must do that. I might go up to the Hall this afternoon and see if I can have a word with her then.'

'Time it right, and she'll have made a cake for tea.'

For a while we ate our sandwich in companionable silence. When I'd finished, I brushed the crumbs from my trousers.

'I came to tell you that I made a decision about your grandmother's party,' I said.

'And?'

'I'll do it,' I said, and saw the relief that sprang into the blue eyes. That made me feel better about it. 'But,' I added firmly, 'we need a plan.'

'Now, why does that not surprise me? Frith, it'll be fine,' he said.

'I'm serious.'

I had been thinking about it ever since he had first suggested that I take my stupid joke to Saffron seriously. It was all very well for George to say that it would all be fine. Some of us had imaginations and could think about all the things that might not be fine at all.

Some of us were spending altogether too much time imagining what it would be like to be George's girlfriend, in fact. There was a jumpy, jittery feeling underneath my skin even when I wasn't thinking about it, and I'd endured another restless night as a result. How had I got myself into this mess? This was what happened when you diverged from your plan.

'We didn't think it through,' I insisted. 'It all seemed easy yesterday. Saffron's wedding, your grandmother's party, that was it. But it's not it, is it? Saffron is coming up to talk about the party soon, and then there's the party itself…'

I was pleating the foil neatly. 'We'll have to get our stories straight so we don't give ourselves away,' I pointed out. 'And what about Roly? Do we tell him what's going on? It's all going to get complicated!'

'I don't see why,' said George. 'All we need to do is pretend to be in love.'

'You're in love with me,' I reminded him quickly. 'I'm just toying with *you.*'

The creases around George's eyes deepened appreciatively. 'You don't think you could be a little in love with me?' he said, looking down at me with glinting blue eyes. 'Letitia would like that. Naturally, I don't mind being toyed with the rest of the time. In fact, any time you feel like toying…'

Oh, God, there went my cheeks again.

'I don't mind making a bit of an effort for her,' I said, concentrating fiercely on the foil, 'but I'm not making a fool of myself in front of Saffron and her friends. That's exactly the kind of thing we ought to sort out now,' I told him.

'Uh-oh, I think I can feel some SMART goals coming on!'

'You're not taking this seriously,' I complained.

'Because it isn't serious,' said George. 'Look, don't worry about it. I'll look at you adoringly and give you a

cuddle every now and then. How much more of a plan do
you want?'

It was the prospect of the cuddles that was worrying me,
but I could hardly admit that to George. *He* clearly hadn't
lost any sleep over how he might react if I kissed him or
slid an arm around him and pressed into his side.

'I still think we should talk about exactly what's involved,' I said stubbornly.

'Tell you what, why don't you come round to supper tomorrow?' said George. 'It's the weekend. We'll have something to eat and we'll make a plan if that makes you happy.'

'I've got a confession to make,' said George when I knocked
on his kitchen door the next evening. 'I've been working
with Toby all day. We were making real progress but, as a
result, I forgot to go to the shops.'

'Does that mean no dinner?'

'Not at all. This is why God invented takeaways,' said
George. 'Pizza or curry?'

It was a filthy night. The spring days had been blown
away by a wind-splattered rain beating angrily against the
cottage windows. I chose curry, and George braved the
weather to drive to the Indian restaurant in the local town,
while I lit the fire in his sitting room.

George's cottage was a mirror image of mine. It had the
same dated décor and shabby furnishings, but it was cosy
in the firelight. I poked the embers and added another log,
thinking that the room was infinitely more inviting than
the most opulent of my father's houses.

We sat on the floor in front of the fire, eating like slobs
straight from the containers and drinking beer from the
bottle.

'So, how are the party preparations coming on?' George
asked. He was lying on one side of the fire, propped on

one elbow, while I leant against an armchair with my legs stretched out in front of me.

I nibbled at an onion bhaji. 'I saw Mrs Simms, and she's absolutely wonderful, just like you said. We talked about a menu, and it all sounds great. I'm clearly going to have a battle with Saffron about the wine, though. We had a big row when I told her I couldn't afford the kind of wines she wants. She wanted me to ask *Dad* to pay for it!

'I was supposed to ring him up and say "Hi, Dad, we haven't spoken for six years, but could you lend me a couple of thousand pounds because I'm too much of a failure to be able to give Saffron the wine she wants at her party?"'

'Hmm, I can see it might be a difficult conversation, but you're hardly a failure, Frith. Nobody's expecting you to earn astronomical sums at this stage of your career.'

'Saffron is. She lives in a different world. Anyway, we agreed in the end that she would pay for the wine, but now, of course, I feel a selfish worm,' I said glumly, and George laughed.

'Frith, you're giving her a party in a stately home. That's generous enough.'

'Only thanks to Roly.'

'You're paying for the food, you're organising it all. You are not a worm,' he said firmly.

Sitting up, he propped himself against the chair opposite mine on the other side of the fire.

Our legs were stretched out side by side. If I moved my left one just a little, it would be pressed up against his right one.

'So you've got the food—and the wine!—sorted now. What else have you got to do?'

'Loads,' I said, 'but I did have a thought about games.'

'Strip poker?' George asked hopefully and I poked him with my foot.

'No, *not* strip poker. It's not going to be that kind of party.'

'Shame.'

'Since Jax is now definitely coming, I thought we could make him and Saffron play Mr and Mrs. It's a sort of test,' I added when George raised his brows enquiringly. He was scraping out the last of the lamb dopiaza and I pushed the container of rice towards him. 'I ask Saffron and Jax a series of questions about each other in advance, and then read out their answers. Then we'll see how well they really know each other.'

'Sounds dangerous to me,' said George. 'What sort of questions were you thinking of?'

'I don't know, what's their favourite book, that kind of thing.' I hadn't given the matter much thought. I wasn't at that stage of planning yet.

'Saffron didn't strike me as a great reader,' he said, which was a tactful way of putting it. My sister had lots of good points, but a razor-sharp intellect wasn't one of them. I had only ever seen her flicking through glossy magazines, and even then I suspected she only looked at the pictures. I couldn't see Jax spending much time buried in a book either.

'Mmm, good point,' I acknowledged. 'What about favourite meal?'

George licked his fork thoughtfully. 'I get it. So if Jax thinks that Saffron's favourite meal is sausage and mash, and she says it's actually a lettuce leaf, hilarity will ensue when you compare their answers.'

'That's the idea.' I hunted round for a pen and turned my list over so that I could write on the back. 'I need some more questions. I thought favourite meal, favourite colour—What?' I broke off as George made a face.

'No self-respecting bloke is going to have a favourite

colour! Why don't you ask something interesting like, what does he/she do when they're nervous?'

I frowned. 'What do you mean?'

'Well, for instance, if *we* were getting married, I'd say that you tucked your hair behind your ears whenever you weren't sure of yourself.'

'I do not!'

'It's a dead giveaway,' said George kindly.

'Or they might ask what your most irritating habit was,' I countered, 'and I would say the way you change my ring-tone *every day*! I got a cow mooing today,' I remembered grouchily. 'You do realise the joke's wearing very thin?

'You promised you wouldn't do it again,' I reminded him crossly. 'Scout's honour, you said. I distinctly remember it.'

'It doesn't count if you were never a scout,' said George. 'Besides, I'm having much too good a time imagining your face when your mobile rings every day.'

'I'll stop using it,' I threatened, but he shook his head.

'Can't be done, Frith. A professional woman like you without a mobile phone? What happens when someone wants to get hold of you and you're on site? No, I think you'll keep it.'

He was right, curse him.

George smiled. He could read my expression without difficulty. 'I'm surprised you haven't worked out how to change it yourself,' he said. 'You being an engineer and all.'

'I deal with big structures,' I said loftily. 'Not all engi-neers are nerds, you know. I've always been hopeless with fiddly technology. I can switch on my computer and send a text, but that's about it.'

'Looks like you're stuck with me choosing your ring-tones, then, doesn't it?'

I rolled my eyes. I wasn't going to let on to George, but actually I did think the ringtones he chose were quite funny.

'As long as you don't pick any more like that first time. It was really embarrassing.'

George paused with the beer bottle at his lips. 'First time,' he echoed. 'Now there's a question for your quiz! Ask Saffron and Jax the name of the first person the other one slept with. It's the sort of thing couples ought to know about each other, isn't it? After all, you never forget your first time, do you?'

I didn't answer, but when George looked at me I realised I had to say something. 'No,' I said.

He nudged me with his foot. 'Go on. What was his name?'

I looked at the flames. I really didn't want to be having this conversation, but George clearly wasn't going to let it go. And I didn't have to make a big deal out of it. It *wasn't* a big deal. Or not any more.

'Charles,' I said.

I thought I said it lightly, but George sat up and put his beer back on the floor. He narrowed his eyes at me.

'Not a good experience?'

'Not particularly.'

That was supposed to be it. I could have left it there. I *should* have left it there. We were only discussing a game, for heaven's sake. But all at once the memories were crowding in my throat, and I was telling George what had happened before I realised that I was going to say anything at all.

'It was awful,' I blurted out.

I fiddled with the corner of the foil dish by my side and didn't look at him. 'It wasn't long after my mother died and I'd had to go and live with my father and Saffron all the time. Saffron was only eight, and Dad was working all the time. I was lonely and missing Mum. I'd gone from a quiet suburban house to a mansion, from a comprehensive to the exclusive private school my father insisted on. I didn't fit in anywhere any more. It wasn't a happy time,' I said. Which might be called a massive understatement.

My father had trodden on a lot of toes on his way to his fortune, and he had never been accepted by the Establishment. He was too brash, too blunt, and he had an enormous chip on his shoulder. I suspected that secretly he longed to be accepted, but he would laugh off any suggestion of it.

'Nobody looks down on you when you've got a few billion in the bank,' he'd boast, but of course among certain circles billions count for nothing when you haven't been to the right school and don't speak with the right accent.

Bullishly, my father tried to force Saffron and I into what he thought of as the 'right' circles, unaware, or perhaps uncaring, that everyone looked down on us. Saffron did better. She went to school with those girls, and grew up with them, and of course she looked the part, but I was never going to belong, and I didn't want to.

'You should make more of an effort,' he ordered me. 'Take your nose out of those books and show those nobs that you're just as good as they are.'

I was horrified when I heard that he had taken a luxurious villa on a private island in the Caribbean for the Christmas holidays and was intent on pushing me into contact with the other young people there. I had nothing to say to them.

And then I met Charles when my father dragged me along to a party at the beach club. To this day, I don't know if he gatecrashed or not, but he was so rich and so confident that it would have taken a brave person to deny him entrance.

'I met him at a party,' I told George. 'I was horribly shy, and embarrassed about my father, and Charles was like

some Greek god, descending from heaven to take notice
of me. He was even more handsome than you,' I said and
George pretended to reel back with shock.

'Impossible!'

'I know it's hard to imagine, but he was. He had that
whole floppy-haired-chiselled-cheek-bones-upper-crust
thing going on, and green eyes like a cat. I was dazzled,'
I admitted.

'I couldn't believe he'd even noticed me, but he flirted
with me and flattered me and for once my father was looking approving. It was so lovely to have some attention,' I
remembered, hating the wistful note in my own voice. 'I
wanted not to be bowled over by Charles, but when he took
my hand and suggested we got away from everybody else,
of course I said yes.'

'I've got a feeling I'm not going to like what comes next,'
said George, an unaccustomed grim look about his mouth.

'You can probably guess. He took me to a dark beach
hut and kissed me and one thing led to another...' I gathered up the foil containers within reach and stacked them
neatly together before I lifted my eyes and looked straight
at George.

'I didn't say no,' I told him firmly. 'I wanted my first
time to be with Charles. He was so gorgeous and glamorous and he made me feel special. Actually, it wasn't that
great. It hurt and was messy and awkward and I didn't have
a clue what I was doing, but for a few minutes there I was
thrilled. It was worth it to be Charles's girlfriend.'

I laughed, but it was a bitter sound. 'He said we should
go back to the party, and he'd leave me to clean myself up.
So he went out and there were a group of his friends waiting outside the hut for him, cheering and clapping him on
the back, and it turned out that he'd won the bet.

'I was the bet.' My cheeks were burning with remembered humiliation. 'It turned out that they'd been taking bets on whether or not he could bang ghastly Kevin Taylor's ghastly daughter, and guess what? He won.' I swallowed. 'I refused to go anywhere for the rest of the time on the island. My father was furious and never forgave me.'

'You didn't tell him what had happened?'

'Of course not. I knew what I was doing. I even wanted it,' I said. 'I wasn't going to cry rape. Besides, I couldn't bear to talk about it. I felt so...*stupid*.'

Had I really thought that someone like Charles would be interested in me? How naïve could you get? At twenty-eight, I could look back and see that Charles had just been a careless boy. He wasn't to know that I was just starting to recover from my mother's death, just beginning to let myself trust again, but at the time I had been devastated. His casual humiliation of me had been all I needed to lock down emotionally, and I had never risked abandoning myself to another person again.

'He hurt you.' George's voice was flat, implacable, and when I glanced at him I saw that the good-humoured face was set so sternly that for a moment I didn't recognise him.

'Everybody gets hurt sooner or later,' I said. 'Even you,' I reminded him, thinking about Annabel. 'Maybe even Charles.'

CHAPTER SIX

GEORGE looked unconvinced, and I was sorry that I'd spoiled the atmosphere.

'Enough of my pathetic story,' I said, trying to lighten the atmosphere. 'I want to hear about your first time now. Fair's fair.'

'If you must know, it was over so quickly I can hardly remember it,' said George, but the grimness had gone from his face and he was clearly following my lead.

'You said we never forgot our first time,' I reminded him.

'All right, her name was Julie.'

'And I bet she was tiny and blonde and wore pretty dresses?'

'Now you come to mention it, I think she *was* blonde,' said George, playing along.

'And pretty, I suppose?'

'I'm afraid so.'

I tsked. 'Why can't you guys ever fall for prickly brunettes who don't know how to talk to boys?' I demanded.

George smiled. 'Who says we don't?'

Outside, the wind shook the windows in frustration and threw rain at the windows in bad-tempered spurts. Inside, a log collapsed into the embers with a soft whump, but otherwise there was just a charged silence.

All at once, the room felt very close, and my skin was

prickling with awareness. My eyes flickered to George's, then away. I picked up the foil container by my knee and put it down again, horribly conscious that I was wearing a ghastly half-smile.

Because I didn't know if he was joking or not. I *thought* he was joking, I was almost sure he was joking, but with George you could never tell. And what would it mean if he *wasn't* joking?

'I've got a plan,' said George.

He had shifted until he was sitting right beside me, his voice so deep that it reverberated along the armchair and into me. I could feel the heat of it quivering deep inside me

'Oh, yes?' I managed. I thought about moving away but that would have made me look cowardly, wouldn't it?

'It's a really good one. I think you'll approve.'

I cleared my throat. 'I like a plan.'

'I hope you'll like this one.'

Very slowly I turned my head until my eyes met his, and my breath snared at his expression.

'What is it?'

'I think we should get into character,' said George. 'If we're going to be really convincing when Saffron comes up next, we'd better rehearse.' He lifted a hand to smooth a stray hair away from my face and my skin burned at his touch. 'What do you think?'

My heart was thudding, my mouth so dry I could hardly speak, and I couldn't have looked away from his eyes if I had tried, but I clung desperately to the shreds of the sensible Frith I knew I really was inside.

'I'm, er, not sure that's really necessary, is it?' I managed somehow.

'I've got a very challenging role,' he pointed out. 'I'm besotted by you, remember? I'm going to have to look as if I know what it's like to slide my hand under your hair, like this,' he said, suiting the action to the words. His palm was warm and persuasive against the nape of my neck. 'I should look as if I know what it's like to nibble your ear lobe and kiss my way down your throat...'

His lips were warm too, so warm, so sure. A great, fluttery rush of heat engulfed me and I sucked in a trembling breath.

'I don't know...'

'As for you,' said George, cupping my cheek to hold my face still, not that I was capable of going anywhere. 'It's going to be even harder for you.'

'It is?'

It was just as well I was sitting down, because I felt boneless with desire. Only the armchair behind me was keeping me upright at all.

'Talk about tough,' he said as he shook his head solemnly. 'You're going to have to look as if you're used to me kissing you. I think you'll need to practise that a lot.'

I was hazy with anticipation. 'I suppose it *might* be an idea to practise a bit,' I heard myself say.

Where was my sensible side when I needed it? It should have been up there on the barricades, repelling all advances, reminding me of all the reasons why kissing George Challoner would be a very bad idea. Instead, it had given up on the fight with barely a murmur of protest and a reckless Frith I hadn't even known existed up to that point was cheering me on.

Go on! Why not kiss him? You know you want to! Be honest now. You know you've been thinking about this ever since you laid eyes on him. He's right, it is quite a good idea. And if he kisses you, it would be rude not to kiss him back, wouldn't it?

And so on.

George smiled. 'That's what I thought,' he said, and

then my lashes were sweeping down as he leant towards me, or maybe I leant towards him, and then his lips pressed against mine. They were warm and firm and oh-so-sure, and the feel of them sent a bolt of intense sensation right through to my toes. I could have sworn the room rocked around me, and I had to put up a hand to George's shoulder to steady myself.

His mouth felt so right that all sensible thought evaporated, and somehow my hand slid round to tangle in his hair to pull him closer and deepen the kiss.

It wasn't a frenzied tonsil-tennis kind of kiss. It was lazier and lovelier than that, almost languorous, at least at first. We leaned into each other and kissed and it was as if we'd kissed a thousand times before. It was like coming home.

I'm not quite sure when it changed. Somehow the lazy pleasure deepened into something more urgent, and, without me meaning it to, my hand came up to his shoulder and then his cheek. I laid my palm against his jaw and felt the graze of his stubble and he smiled against my mouth.

'Pretty good,' he said. 'But I'm not sure we got it *quite* right. We'd better try again.'

So we did, sliding down onto the carpet as I abandoned myself to the sheer pleasure of kissing and being kissed while the excitement raced between us, ratcheting up a notch with each touch, each kiss, each press of our bodies.

Our hands grew hungrier, our kisses more demanding. My arms came up so that I could tug George's shirt from his trousers, so I could slide my palms over his broad, strong back. He felt wonderful. His skin was warm and smooth, and I could feel the powerful muscles flex under my touch.

His hands were everywhere, hot and wickedly persuasive, discovering me, unlocking me, undoing me, and I arched beneath him, incoherent words tumbling from my lips.

'Frith,' he murmured, rolling over me.

That was when he knocked over the beer bottle.

The splash brought me to my senses. I froze as the pool of liquid spread beneath me, and then I struggled up, pushing George away. 'What are we *doing*?' I said, flustered.

'We're kissing,' he said and reached for me again, but I scooted out of his way.

'I think we should stop,' I said with difficulty. 'Maybe it wasn't such a good idea after all.'

'What do you mean? It was a brilliant idea. The best I've ever had.'

It was typical of George that he wasn't in the least self-conscious, unlike me. I was acutely aware of my tousled hair and swollen lips, of the imprint of George's hands on my thigh, his lips on my throat. I fumbled with my buttons. How had *they* come undone?

'Maybe that's enough practice,' I said. 'We don't want to get carried away.'

'Don't we?'

'All right, *I* don't,' I said. 'I don't want to forget this is just a pretence.'

George leant back on his elbow and regarded me thoughtfully. 'This is about Charles, isn't it?'

'No,' I said instinctively, then honesty made me consider the question. 'Well, maybe it's a bit about him.'

'You don't trust me,' said George.

'I do! That is…I think I do. It's not about you, or me,' I tried to explain. I was trying to mop up the beer and fasten my blouse at the same time, with a spectacular lack of success in both cases. 'I just don't think we should…get serious,' I said.

There was a silence. I could feel George's blue gaze on my face, but I couldn't look at him. 'It was only a kiss,' he said eventually.

Only a kiss. Only a kiss that had rocked me off my axis, that had left my skin twitching and my blood roaring and my heart slamming in my chest.

'We both know we wouldn't have stopped if you hadn't knocked over that beer,' I said.

'I'll be more careful next time,' said George.

'There won't be a next time,' I said firmly. I had managed to do up my blouse by then and was feeling more under control.

'What about Saffron's party?' he said after a moment. 'Don't I get to kiss you then? After all, you were the one who told Saffron I can't keep my hands off you,' he reminded me. 'And it would be a shame to put all this practice to waste!'

What had ever made me think I could get away with pretending to be sleeping with George? I wondered, smoothing my hair back and eyeing him in frustration. He just wasn't taking this seriously, but then, why was I surprised? George didn't take anything seriously.

The whole idea was mad, I could see that now, but it was too late to back out. I could just imagine the hard time George would give me if I tried! Somehow, though, I had to wrestle things back under control.

'We can kiss if necessary,' I said stiffly, 'but not like… you know…the way we just did. It's not as if Saffron or your grandmother will expect us to get it on in front of everybody else, is it? That's not how people behave.'

George linked his hands behind his head and leant back into the chair. 'Frith Taylor, I do believe you're embarrassed!'

'Of course I'm embarrassed!' I snapped. 'I don't usually let things get out of hand like that.'

'It's not so bad letting go, is it?'

'Yes,' I said, still reeling with how close I had come to

throwing myself back into that abyss where I flailed out of control. 'I don't like it. I know you're going to tell me I'm repressed, but that's just the way I am.'

'You weren't repressed when you were kissing me just now.'

I was glad of the dim light that hid the colour that swept up my throat at the mere memory of that kiss.

'No, well, that was out of character,' I mumbled.

'Not getting carried away can't make your relationships much fun,' said George.

Why couldn't he just let the subject drop? I eyed him crossly. 'My relationships have been fine,' I said. 'My boy-friends were like me. They didn't want an intense relation-ship either.' It was true enough. All three had had a prosaic approach that I found reassuring. That was why we'd got together in the first place. 'None of them wanted to get too involved,' I told George, 'and I didn't either.'

George dropped his hands. He wasn't smiling any more. 'Because if you were too involved, you might feel some-thing? And if you felt something, he might hurt you, the way Charles did? The way your father did?'

'This isn't about my father,' I said coldly. 'I don't need to be psychoanalysed, George. I'm just explaining that I'm a woman who knows what she wants, and what I want is to be in control of my life. Frankly, I don't see anything wrong with that.'

My lips tightened when George just shook his head.

'Look, the fact is that we're completely different,' I told him. 'It's not as if a relationship between us could go any-where even if we wanted one. You're committed to your life here, and I'll be leaving as soon as Hugh is better.'

'You know, not every good relationship has to last for ever,' said George. 'Neither of us is involved with anyone else. We could have a good time until you go, but you won't even consider that because being spontaneous and having a good time isn't in your plan!'

'Maybe I won't consider it because I don't *want* it,' I snapped back. 'You're not nearly as irresistible as you think you are. I'm not saying what just happened wasn't pleasant, and I'm just as responsible as you are for letting it go too far, but I don't want to do it again.'

I certainly wasn't going to tell George that I was afraid that if we kissed again I wouldn't be able to stop myself getting involved. I might have told him that my previous relationships had been fine, but of course they hadn't. I deliberately chose men who wouldn't push me for commitment, men I could hold at arm's length.

Men with whom there was never, frankly, much danger of getting carried away.

There was more than a smidgeon of truth in George's analysis, which was why it had stung. Not that I was going to tell him that either.

'I just don't think it would be a good idea for us to get any more involved than we are already,' I told George. 'I'm happy for us to be friends, and to help each other out as we agreed, but that's it.'

'No more practising?' said George. He had put on a downcast expression, but in the firelight I could see that his eyes were dancing, and it strengthened my resolve. What was it about me that he found so damn funny anyway?

'No,' I said. 'No practising. I can't answer for your grandmother, but it's not as if it's going to take any great acting to convince Saffron that we're a couple anyway,' I added. 'She'll see what she wants to see.'

The truth of this was borne out a couple of weeks later when Saffron came up to see how preparations for the party were progressing.

I cooked supper for her in my cottage, and invited George and Roly. It wasn't what Saffron was used to, of course, but she entered gamely into the spirit of the occasion.

I'm not much of a cook, as I think I've mentioned before, but I made spaghetti bolognese, which wasn't too bad, even though I says it as shouldn't. George and Roly certainly seemed to appreciate it. Saffron was horrified at the idea of pasta, of course, but seemed happy to pick at the salad, and, having got her own way over the wine, had clearly set out to be charming.

George and I tried to explain the Mr and Mrs game to her, but it was hard going.

'So if Frith and I were the couple, for instance, you'd ask me what Frith likes in her sandwiches,' George tried, 'and I'd say cheese and chutney.'

'Whereas, in fact, my favourite sandwich is cheese and salad,' I put in.

George shook his head definitely. 'You only *think* you like salad,' he said. 'Actually, you prefer chutney.'

I opened my mouth to argue but saw that Saffron was looking bewildered. 'But I don't know what Jax likes,' she said. 'And I don't eat sandwiches.'

'That was just an example,' I said, shooting a warning glance at George. 'There are lots of others. What's Jax's pet peeve, for instance? George can't bear a dirty dishwasher. You'd never think it to look at him, but he's really quite anal that way.'

'Hey, pot, look who's talking anal!' He turned confidentially to Saffron. 'If you want to drive Frith wild, leave a drawer open just a bit. Works every time!'

Saffron bit her bottom lip, her perfect brow creased with the effort of thought. 'Jax doesn't like bad reviews,' she confided at last.

I suppressed a sigh. 'It's really about more intimate things than that, Saffron. Does Jax know what brand of moisturiser you use? Does he know how you take your tea? Does he remember what you were wearing when you first met?'

'I was in a John Galliano yellow dress.' Saffron remembered her own wardrobe, but I wondered how much notice Jax had taken.

It worried me that the two of them seemed to spend so little time together, but, as George kept saying, they were old enough to make their own decisions.

'What was Frith wearing?' Saffron asked George unexpectedly. I thought it would put him on the spot, but he answered promptly.

'Oh, that's easy. It was raining, and she was standing in the mud in a jacket and boots and a yellow hard hat, but still managing to look cool and crisp and elegant. I noticed that straight back of hers first of all, and then she turned and put her chin up when she saw me.'

Saffron clapped her hands together. 'Was it love at first sight?'

'I wouldn't say that,' said George, playing up to his role magnificently. 'She looked cross at first. She had her lips folded together, the way she does. You know?' He demonstrated for Saffron, exaggerating madly of course, and she giggled in recognition. 'Still, I thought she was really pretty, and I asked her out, and she said no.'

'You didn't?' Saffron gaped at me in disbelief.

'I didn't want to be a notch in George's bedpost,' I said. 'And really, I had better things to do.'

George exchanged a look with Saffron. 'Frith didn't make it easy for me, I have to admit,' he said. 'She's a hard woman, but then, I've always liked a challenge, and the more I saw her, the more intrigued I was. I know she's not obvious, but she's got the most lovely eyes—have you noticed that?'

'I suppose they *are* unusual,' Saffron agreed, turning to stare at my face.

'They're like ditchwater,' I mumbled, forgetting my role as insatiable man-eater in my embarrassment.

'Ditchwater? They're the most beautiful hazel,' George insisted. 'They're the clearest eyes I've ever seen,' he added, looking straight into them, and for a moment there were just the two of us, and my pulse tumbling in my ear.

'Ah-h-h,' said Saffron.

'And her hair!' George recollected himself, lifting a few strands from my shoulder. 'It's gorgeous, isn't it?'

'It's brown,' I said, rolling my eyes, but he shook his head.

'You think it's brown when you first see it, but when you look closer, you can see honey and gold and melted butter.'

'Oh, please!'

'No, he's right,' said Roly, to my surprise. I hadn't thought he had noticed anything except Saffron. 'It's really pretty.'

'That's the thing about Frith,' George confided to the others, smoothing my hair back into place, and ignoring my attempts to kick him under the table. 'You take a first look and you see one thing, but when you look again, you see more, and every time you look at her, she seems more beautiful.'

I cleared my throat. 'Gosh, George, I didn't know you were a poet.'

'It's true. You think you're ordinary, but you're not. You're just not obvious, and I think you do that deliberately.'

'I've always thought Frith didn't make enough of herself,' Saffron agreed.

'Anyone for more pasta?' I asked brightly.

'It's difficult to pin down just what it is that attracts us to someone else, isn't it?' George spoke across me to Saffron. 'Take Frith's features one by one, and, yes, maybe they're not that special, but put them together into Frith, and I can lose my mind just thinking about what she feels like.' He turned to me with his glinting blue smile. 'And when I make her smile, I feel like I've conquered Everest.'

'Ah, sweet!' said Saffron.

'George, Saffron isn't interested in this,' I said with another kick under the table. I was very much *not* smiling.

'You shouldn't be embarrassed about George wanting you, Frith,' said Saffron. 'It's lovely to see how much you love each other.'

I opened my mouth to inform her that there was no danger of me being in love with George when I caught his eye and remembered the deal we had made, and shut it again.

'Frith's a behind-closed-door woman,' George told Saffron. 'But don't let that cool exterior fool you. Inside, she's a wild woman, aren't you, Tiger?'

I pushed at his shoulder, and he pretended to topple over. 'Ignore him, Saffron,' I said. 'And as for you,' I said severely to George, 'you're to behave yourself or I won't take you to Saffron's wedding.'

'Oh, no, you must come!' exclaimed Saffron. She turned to Roly with a sweet smile. 'And you'll come too, won't you, Roly? I'd love to see you on my special day.'

Roly turned pink. 'I'd be honoured,' he said.

Once George had stopped his ridiculously over-the-top performance, it turned into a surprisingly enjoyable evening, and nobody seemed to care that the wine was on special offer.

I'd been nervous that Roly might not be able to play along—he was a darling, but not the sharpest crayon in the box, it had to be said—but I needn't have worried. When Saffron was in the room, he didn't notice what anyone else was doing anyway. He sat and gazed adoringly at her and, as Saffron was more than happy to sit and be adored, the two of them needed little entertaining, which left George and I to bicker as normal.

Whatever normal was. I wasn't sure any more.

That month in Whellerby, I thought of my life as two halves: Before Kiss and After Kiss. Most of the time, I longed to go back to how I was before that kiss, when I had been focused and in control and my life was proceeding perfectly according to my five-year plan. I flayed myself endlessly for having given into temptation, for letting George kiss me. For kissing him back.

What a stupid, brainless thing to do! Because now, of course, I couldn't get the memory of it out of my head.

In spite of everything I'd had to say to George about wanting to forget that it had ever happened, I couldn't.

Too many times during the day, I'd find my mind drifting away from timescales and local authority regulations or where to source recycled cellulose insulation, away from the things I should be thinking about to George and how he had kissed me.

I'd sit at my computer and stare at an elevation on screen, and instead of picturing the finished building I'd think about how George had smiled at me in the firelight. I'd remember the wicked pleasure of his mouth, the insistent roam of his hands. I'd remember the ripple of muscles in his back and the feel of his sleek, strong body pressed into mine, and my mouth would dry and my pulse would start a dull thudding.

Too many times at night I'd have to give myself a stern lecture entitled Don't Be Stupid. I had a plan, I reminded myself, and it didn't involve making a fool of myself over any man, especially not one as unsuitable as George. I was focusing on my career for the next five years. There would be time enough to think about a sensible relationship after that, and it wasn't going to be with someone who thought it was funny to mess around with my phone and who couldn't sit on a chair properly.

Annoyingly, George himself didn't seem to be having any problems at all carrying on as if nothing whatsoever had happened. I saw him every day. He'd turn up at the site with a sandwich for me, and wait for me to scold him about the latest ringtone he had installed.

Somehow he managed to change it every day. I never knew what my phone was going to sound like. I had snarling tigers and barking dogs, I had bells and whistles and blaring sirens. I had the theme tune to *Hawaii Five-O*, I had the national anthem. I had Elvis Presley and Elvis Costello, Beethoven and Bach, splats and whoopee cushions. I had stupid voices and sexy voices and once an angelic choirboy whose pure tones made me want to cry.

I still have no idea where he got them all from, but the men on the site loved them. They vied with each other to guess what the next day's ringtone would be, and if no one else rang my mobile when I was on the site they would call me themselves just to see what absurd sound emerged from my pocket.

I saw George almost every evening too. He'd let himself into my cottage and cajole me into going for a drink, or to keep Roly company up at the Hall. Invariably Mrs Simms had cooked a delicious supper, so that was a popular choice. The three of us would ignore our grand surroundings and hole up in Roly's private sitting room instead, watching television or arguing. Well, George and I argued. I suspect Roly tuned us out and dreamt of Saffron.

George teased me and irritated me and made me laugh,

and somewhere along the line we became the friends I'd said I wanted to be.

Again and again, I told myself that was enough. I told myself it was all for the best. But every time I looked at George's mouth, my mind would go hot and dark for a moment. If I brushed against him while we were sitting in the pub or slumped together on Roly's sofas, every cell in my body would jitter with longing, and my pulse would jump and throb in sympathy.

I was exasperated with myself. I had *decided*. I was sticking to my plan. There was absolutely no point in thinking about it any more.

And yet more and more I found myself remembering what George had said about making the most of my time in Whellerby. Treacherous thoughts kept sneaking in, undermining my sternest resolution. Why *not* treat it as a lighthearted affair? I didn't have to do anything rash like falling in love. I couldn't afford to do that and, besides, that wasn't the point. It would be a purely physical relationship, I persuaded myself. Surely I could keep things superficial? It wasn't as if George would want to get embroiled in a passionate affair either.

The trouble was, having made such a stand about that kiss, I couldn't think of a way to raise the subject with him. I didn't do flirting or seduction. I was sure Saffron would have been able to let him know that she had changed her mind without saying a word, but every time I thought about starting the conversation, I lost my nerve.

It wasn't just finding the words. I'd no sooner decided that I would say something to George than all my old insecurities would come tumbling back. Why should George want me? He had probably just been amusing himself when he kissed me. It wasn't even as if I were his type. If we went to the pub, he'd pretend to be disappointed that he was stuck with me when I pointed out all the pretty girls there he ought to get to know, as they were bound to be so much more suitable than I was, but I suspected I had become a challenge for him.

I had been a challenge for Charles too.

Not that George was like Charles. We were friends. I knew he liked me, but what if he was bored with me the moment the challenge was won? Worse, what if I was a terrible disappointment in bed? In spite of all my boasting about all the 'fine' relationships I'd had in the past, I wasn't very experienced. I was afraid I wouldn't match up to the sweet-sexy-fun Annabels of this world.

I went round and round in circles of longing, doubt and frustration, winding myself up into such a state that I was actually glad of the distraction when the weekend of Saffron's party arrived.

Saffron and her friends spilled out of their cars with much shrieking and squealing and showing off of perfect cheekbones. I'd met some of them before, but honestly found it hard to tell them apart. They were all called things like Feathers or Jinx, and spent a lot of time dragging their hands through their hair, omigodding when they saw the Hall and making play with their lashes.

And that was just the men.

As a group they were impossibly glamorous. There was a glossiness to them, a sort of nervous energy that set me on edge. I felt like a sturdy pony shoved into a field full of racehorses.

I felt sixteen again, and as excluded from the in-crowd as I had been when Charles decided he could have some fun with me.

But Saffron was happy, and Jax turned up in time for the dinner. That was all that mattered, I told myself.

The Hall looked wonderful. It had been open to the public since Easter and every surface gleamed. The beds in the east wing had all been aired, and preparations for the elaborate dinner were under way in the kitchen.

After discussion with Mrs Simms, I had kept the decoration to fresh flowers, as befitted the Edwardian theme of the weekend. There were great bowls of peonies in the centre of the polished mahogany dining table, and vases of larkspur and phlox massed in the long gallery where the party had gathered for pre-dinner cocktails. It was a beautiful May evening, and the long windows in the gallery were open onto the south terrace with its view down over the lake.

George had volunteered to be a footman but Saffron wouldn't hear of it. 'You and Roly are guests,' she said. 'I can't have my sister's boyfriend waiting at table!'

Unfortunately that meant I had to be a guest too, although I would much rather have kept an eye on things behind the scenes. I was fairly sure none of the guests would know if I was at the party or not, and I'd thought that if George and I could have been staff, it would have been a lot more fun. But George was only allowed to make the cocktails—we weren't pushing authenticity too far—and I had to be content with popping in and out of the party to see how things were going on downstairs.

CHAPTER SEVEN

EVERYONE had taken the Edwardian theme to heart. I've no idea where they got their costumes from, but they all looked ravishing. The men wore white tie and tails, while the girls were in a dazzling array of evening gowns, out-peacocking each other in long gloves and jewels that glimmered at their throats and in their ears.

Guess who was odd one out? My dress was very simple, made of sage-coloured silk with short sleeves that draped and an elegant neckline that left rather more of my shoulders exposed than was advisable in the draughty dining room. Still, I had nothing like the flesh on display in some of the other dresses. Saffron herself was dazzling in a midnight blue beaded creation with narrow straps and a deep V at the back. It was the perfect foil for her bright blonde hair, and Roly couldn't take his eyes off her.

Next to my sister, I looked like the poor relation I was, but at least I had the satisfaction of knowing that my dress was genuine. Roly had suggested that I look in the attics, where I found whole trunkfuls of clothes, and Mrs Simms, whom I was recommending for canonisation, helped me alter it. It did the job of making me invisible, which was exactly what I wanted, and I was able to slip away to the kitchens and check that everything was under control there without anyone noticing.

Roly had taken away the heavy red ropes that normally kept the public away from the furniture in the long gallery. I was nervous about people dropping their drinks or breaking some of the spindlier looking chairs, but he waved aside my concerns.

'The rooms were built to be lived in,' he reminded me. 'It's great to see the house being used the way it was meant to.'

Saffron was the sparkling centre of the party, in her element as the focus of attention. I was pleased to see her looking so happy. We had decided in the end to drop the idea of the Mr and Mrs quiz. Saffron had been able to answer so few of the questions we'd planned that I was afraid it might turn out to expose a ghastly distance between the two of them. But for tonight at least Jax was the perfect fiancé, looking darkly handsome and dropping hints about being in the running for the next James Bond.

'Everybody! Everybody, listen up!' I was about to slip back to the kitchen—I knew Mrs Simms was worried about her lobster bisque—when Saffron swooped down on me and enfolded me in her scented embrace. 'Come with me,' she said, and dragged me to the centre of the room where she proceeded to make an extravagant speech thanking me for the party, and telling me that I was the best sister in the world.

I was touched, but wished that she would stop. I was bright red, and I could see some of the guests looking at each other and mouthing *That's* Saffron's *sister?*

Saffron had clearly had one too many cocktails already. 'I love you, Frith,' she finished owlishly, and I remembered the little girl who had clung to my hand, not understanding why her big sister was so unhappy.

'I love you too, Saffron,' I said, my throat suddenly tight.

Everybody was looking at us, not knowing what to do next. I caught sight of Jax, looking pained.

'Jax, come here,' I said, beckoning him into the spotlight where he belonged with Saffron, and, inspired by desperation, I made a short speech on the spot so that everyone could drink to their happiness. This was a good move, as it enabled me to slink away to where George was making cocktails at the back of the room. He had a shaker in both hands and was shaking it with aplomb. Anyone would think he'd spent his entire life as a barman.

For a moment, I just stood and watched him. If I'd thought he looked good in muddy boots and jeans, in white tie and tails he was heart-stopping. My stomach had hollowed whenever I caught sight of him through the crowd. No one looking at him that night would guess that this was a man who spent his spare time coaxing a damaged horse back to health, who sat in the site office with his feet on my desk, or shared a sandwich on the stable block.

Instead, he looked utterly at home. George belonged with my sister's glossy crowd in a way I never could, I thought dully. He might want a nice country girl, but this had been his life once. Looking at these beautiful girls, these people who had nothing to do all day but have a good time, how could he not miss it?

How could he possibly be interested in having an affair with an uptight engineer? I cringed at the idea that I had been even thinking of asking him. I didn't fit here, and I didn't fit with him. It was just as well I'd remembered that in time, before I made a complete fool of myself.

George handed two margaritas to the girls who had been eyeing him under their lashes with a smile that made my heart twist in my chest. They wandered off back into the party, and he turned back to the temporary bar he'd set up

on a cloth-covered table. I didn't manage to turn away in
time, and he caught me watching him.

'That was a nice speech,' he said, sounding so exactly the
way he always did that I was thrown. He looked so at home
that he ought by rights to be speaking with a languid drawl.

'The evening was supposed to be about Saffron and Jax,
not me.' I felt stiff and uneasy with him, although George
didn't seem to notice anything amiss.

'Still, I'm glad she thanked you. Do you think she has
any idea how hard you've worked for this party?'

'Mrs Simms has done most of the work,' I said. 'I'm
sending her a huge bunch of flowers tomorrow.'

George wiped the shaker with a cloth. 'Well, it looks
like the party's a big success already. You can stop worrying now.'

'I just hope they don't damage anything.' I clutched my
elbows, surveying the guests with a tense frown. 'They're
already well away. Can you make those cocktails a bit
weaker? They'll be too sloshed to appreciate Mrs Simms's
cooking otherwise and I'll have humiliated myself for nothing.'

'Relax,' said George soothingly. 'They're enjoying themselves. That's what they're supposed to be doing.'

'That's what's worrying me,' I snapped. 'This place is
chock-a-block with valuable antiques. Do you really want
them covered with glass rings?'

'You are such a worrywart,' George said, exasperated.
'Stop fretting and look adoring. We're supposed to be having a mad, passionate affair.'

'It's not that kind of affair,' I reminded him. Reminded
myself. 'I'm just amusing myself with you, remember?' I
was on edge, and it wasn't just the prospect of ring marks
on Roly's heirlooms. I couldn't believe I had wasted so
much time even considering an affair with someone like

George. Hadn't I learnt my lesson with Charles all those years ago? '*You* adore *me*.'

Like *that* was a likely scenario.

'So I do,' said George, putting down the shaker and reaching for me before I had time to resist. 'I think it's time I got into lovesick-puppy mode, don't you?'

His arm was warm and strong around my waist as he held me to him, and he kissed me, his mouth smiling against mine. He was gloriously solid, his lips wickedly enticing. For one treacherous moment I longed to relax into him.

Not fit? *This is where you fit!* my body was shouting. *You fit right here.*

But that couldn't be right. I was the one who never fitted anywhere. Not here, not with George. I tried to pull away but he held me tight. 'We don't need to do this,' I said tensely. 'No one's the slightest bit interested in us and Saffron's not watching.'

'I know,' said George. 'Maybe I feel like a lovesick puppy anyway.'

I glanced at him uncertainly, only to find my eyes snared in those impossibly blue ones. The long gallery rang with chatter and squeals of laughter, but the two of us were trapped in a bubble of stillness and silence, where there was nothing but the blueness of George's eyes and the thump of my heart and the warmth on my skin where he held me.

His gaze was so warm, it was reeling me in, and in spite of my tension, in spite of everything I'd just decided, I was swaying towards him when our bubble was rudely punctured.

'I say.'

One of the guests—Clive, I seemed to remember Saffron introducing him as—was lurching towards us. I jumped and would have sprung away from George if he hadn't clamped a hand on my waist and secured me back against him.

'We're lovers,' he murmured in my ear. 'I can't keep my hands off you, remember?'

I laughed a little nervously. If we hadn't been interrupted when we had, I was very much afraid that I might have been the one who couldn't keep my hands to myself. I turned to Clive with a mixture of gratitude and frustration.

He had a cut-glass accent, patrician cheekbones and the requisite floppy hair, but a dissolute air clung to him, and I wondered if this was what George had been like once.

I hoped Clive didn't want another cocktail. It was obvious that he was already half-cut.

But it turned out that Clive had something else on his mind. 'I say,' he said again, weaving up to us and poking a wavering finger into George's chest. 'Didn't you used to be George Challoner?'

George stiffened, but he kept his smile easy. 'Once upon a time,' he said.

'Told you, Jon!' Clive chortled and turned to the friend who was swaying gently beside him. 'It is him!'

'George Challoner, a barman?' the other guy said, frowning in concentration. He shook his head so vehemently that he staggered, and I could only watch in horror as he reeled towards a delicate eighteenth-century side table. At the very last moment, he hauled himself upright. 'Don't believe it!' he said.

'I prefer to think of myself as a cocktail provider,' said George. 'It sounds better, don't you think?'

'From Challoners to barman…bit of a comedown, isn't it?'

'That depends how you look at it,' said George pleasantly.

Clive was staring at him hard, presumably to stop his eyes crossing. 'I thought you were in prison,' he said.

At that, George let me go. 'No,' he said. 'It seems not.'

'I worked for Challoners, you know,' Clive slurred. 'You don't remember me, but I was there. It was my first job, and I was having a great time. Then suddenly there are cutbacks and retrenchments and the Serious Fraud Office are called in, and guess what? It was all because of *you*. I was out of a job and I'd missed my chance to get in with other investment banks. Do you have any idea how humiliating that was?'

His face twisted with resentment. 'I don't suppose you gave a thought to the people who would lose out because of you?'

'I've got to admit,' said George in a level voice, 'that I wasn't thinking of you at all.' He glanced at Clive's immaculately tailored dinner jacket, at the Rolex on his wrist. 'You seem to have done all right in spite of me.'

'Eventually,' Clive conceded. 'Not as well as you, though, obviously,' he added, turning his bleary gaze to me.

I didn't need him to tell me what he saw: I was trim and dull and totally unspectacular. 'Not a bad move hooking up with one of Kevin Taylor's daughters, eh?'

The subtext was obvious: what use would any man have for me if it weren't for my father's fabled millions?

'Never even knew Saffron had a sister,' Clive went on, oblivious to the dangerous look on George's face. 'Now I see why you're hiding away in the country.'

George didn't say anything, but his expression blazed with such contempt that even in their befuddled state the two men took an unsteady step backwards. My mouth dried as I watched George. I'd never seen him lose his temper before, and he made me think of nothing so much as a big cat, tail twitching, muscles coiled to lash out with a snarl.

The confrontation was beginning to attract attention. I saw Saffron turn, and I laid my hand on George's arm.

'George,' I said warningly.

George didn't look at me, but I could feel the rigidity in his arm relax very slightly after a moment when he re-alised that a scene would spoil things for Saffron. I saw the effort it took to release his jaw, where a muscle still twitched dangerously.

'Excuse me,' he said, picking up the tray of glasses from the table behind him. 'There are guests needing drinks out there.'

As he passed Clive he said something in his ear. I didn't catch it, but I saw Clive's expression darken. Whatever it was, it hadn't been nice.

'You be careful,' Clive said to me savagely as he caught me watching him. 'George Challoner's a bad lot. Everybody knows that.'

To my dismay, I found myself sitting next to Clive's friend, Jon, at the dinner. Saffron had done the seating plan, on the grounds that I wouldn't know who would want to sit together and who needed to be kept apart. I'd been more than happy to let her agonise over it, but now I wished I'd paid more attention. George was right at the other end of the table.

Jon had clearly decided to appoint himself my advisor.

'How much do you know about George Challoner?' he asked me in a low voice as we unfolded our linen napkins and he splashed wine into my glass.

'Enough,' I said.

'I couldn't believe it when I saw him here.' Jon took a reviving slurp of wine. 'I said to Clive, I thought he was in prison. He should be!' He shook his head. 'Does Saffron know he was fired?'

'I don't think being sacked is a criminal offence yet,' I said coldly.

'It is when you're doing what George Challoner was

doing. Corruption is a serious business and he was embezzling hedge funds.'

I wasn't going to let him know that I didn't know what
hedge funds were.

'Since he didn't go to prison, it's safe to assume that he
didn't do it,' I said.

'The Challoners hushed it up as much as they could,
but the Serious Fraud Office were there for months. It was
catastrophic for their reputation as a bank and as a family,'
said Jon. 'It's them I feel sorry for. One black sheep, and the
whole family gets tarred with the same brush. My people
know the Challoners and they've really suffered because
of what George did.'

My eyes found George at the other end of the table. He
was laughing with the girl next to him, and he looked so
at ease, so at home, that my heart clenched. I wanted him
to be in my office—yes, even tipped back on the chair!—
with his thick socks and his old jacket, not here, looking
like the star of some costume drama.

He had never told me what had really caused the estrangement with his family. Oh, he'd admitted to being
sacked, but I'd assumed that was because of his party lifestyle more than anything else. Embezzlement sounded more
serious but George…corrupt? I didn't believe it.

Once he realised I wasn't going to thank him for re-
vealing George's sordid history, Jon lost interest in me,
and spent the rest of the evening with his shoulder turned
to me while he talked to the group on his right, roaring
with laughter every now and then to show me what I was
missing.

Once I caught George's eye and he mouthed *All right?*
Immediately I put on a brilliant smile and nodded and pretended to be immersed in conversation with the man on
my left, who was so dull I really can't remember his name.

We'd agreed that people would help themselves to wine, but I noticed it was George who got up every now and then and opened new bottles or went round topping up glasses. Most of the men treated him as a servant, either ignoring him completely, or covering their glasses impatiently with their hands rather than go to the trouble of saying, 'No, thank you.'

George gave no indication that he noticed their rudeness, but I burned with humiliation on his behalf. I'd thought he looked at home, but it hadn't occurred to me that he'd been estranged from this life as well as his family. It had to be difficult for him to face it again, especially now he had been recognised. Clive had clearly been busy and word had got round. I saw several of the men look at him askance.

The dinner dragged on, course after course. Saffron had wanted a 'real' Edwardian dinner, so we had the lobster bisque, and then sole Véronique. Mushroom vol-au-vents, Yorkshire beef, guinea fowl, rose-petal water ice, strawberry galette, savouries...I thought it would never end. Mrs Simms had excelled herself, but I would happily have stopped with the fish dish. The sheer amount of food felt grotesque.

Everyone else seemed to be having a great time, though, and the table was cluttered with empty wine bottles. Saffron had taken advice from some friend of hers who claimed to be a wine expert, and had spent an astronomical sum on wines to go with the meal, but I didn't see one person look at the labels or exclaim at how delicious it was. I had a couple of glasses—I needed it to get through the evening—and it was very good, but I didn't think it was that much better than the wine we had at the cottage, which was on special offer at the supermarket.

I could hardly move by the time the last savouries had been eaten, the port passed, and the party moved away

from the table at last and spilled out onto the terrace outside the long gallery. I took the opportunity to slip away
to the kitchens and help Mrs Simms and the niece she'd
roped in from the village to give her a hand. I didn't think
anyone would notice that I'd gone, and, to be honest, I had
a much better time gossiping with them than I had done
being cold-shouldered by Jon.

I planned to walk home. I'd had a bit to drink and it was
a beautiful evening. When I'd thanked Mrs Simms, I wandered outside from the kitchens at the side of the house. I'd
have to say goodbye to Saffron, but I couldn't face the noise
of the party again just yet. The last time I'd seen George,
he'd had two blondes draped over him. Ostracised by the
men or not, he'd obviously been coping with the dinner and
the company better than I had.

My shoes were pinching horribly and my back ached
from unfamiliar heels. I actually groaned when I reached
the grass and could take the shoes off. Holding them in
one hand, I wandered away around the back of the house.
The lawn was cool and comforting beneath my bare feet,
and above the sky was a deep, dark blue. From the terrace
at the front I could hear the party continuing, but there at
the back it was quiet and still.

Two vast stone urns marked the bottom of a flight of
wide steps that led down from the back terrace, and as I
rounded one, absently trailing my fingers over the mossy
stone, a voice spoke from the dimness of the steps above
me, and I just about leapt out of my skin.

'Had enough too?'

'George!' I patted my throat to push my heart back into
place. 'I thought you were having a good time with the
others.'

His face was too shadowy for me to read his expression. 'No. I looked for you when everyone left the table, but you'd gone.'

'I just went down to the kitchen to thank Mrs Simms.' I felt stupidly shy. 'What are you doing out here?'

'Oh…thinking,' he said. 'What about you?'

'Trying to persuade my feet that they will go into shoes again one day.'

'Come and sit down.' George patted the step beside him.

I didn't want him to think I was avoiding him because of anything Clive had said, so I climbed up, still barefoot, and sat beside him. Dropping my shoes onto the step below, I copied George, and rested my folded arms on my knees.

The night smelt of summer, of lush grass and soft air. I drew a lungful and let it out slowly. 'It's nice out here. Peaceful.'

George nodded. 'I don't know how anyone would prefer to live in London,' he said. 'Why would you want a big city when you could have this?'

'I was watching you this evening,' I said. 'In spite of Clive, you looked so at home with those people.' I hesitated. 'I wondered if tonight had been hard for you. I wondered if you were thinking about the life you had before you came here, if you missed it at all.'

George gave a short laugh. 'Do I miss it? Hardly! I was just sitting here wondering how I stood that life for so long. I hate the idea that I was that idle and mindless and self-absorbed, but I was.'

There was a bleakness to his voice I hadn't heard before, and I didn't like it. Without thinking, I laid my hand on his arm.

'You're not like that now,' I said. 'I wonder if you ever were.'

'I was pretty unpleasant,' said George. 'You wouldn't

have liked me at all.' But he covered my hand with his own, turning it over so that our fingers laced together.

'I suppose Jon has told you all my dirty secrets over dinner?'

'He told me that you were sacked for embezzling hedge funds.'

'Aren't you going to ask me if I did it or not?'

'No,' I said calmly. 'You can be deeply irritating at times, and the way you mess with my ringtone is probably downright illegal, but I don't see you as an embezzler somehow.'

George's fingers tightened around mine. 'I've got a braying donkey for you next,' he said with a half-smile.

'I can't wait.'

There was a pause. The party round the front were growing raucous but here in the back the quiet summer night wrapped us in a warm cocoon.

'I didn't go to prison,' George said abruptly, letting go of my hand. 'I don't know what that is—a rumour? wishful thinking?—but it isn't true.'

'I didn't think it was,' I said. 'What did happen, George? If you didn't do anything illegal, why are you estranged from your family?'

'I broke ranks,' he said, 'I didn't play the game the way I was supposed to.'

He was silent so long I thought he wasn't going to say any more. I was very conscious of him beside me, the starlight skimming the lines of his face and throat. He'd unbuttoned his collar and his tie hung around his neck, and the whiteness of his shirt gleamed in the darkness. I wanted to touch him, to tell him that I didn't care what he'd done, but I made myself stay silent and let him tell the story in his own time.

'It's ironic that I only ran into trouble the one time I

tried to do my job,' he said at last, hunching forward as if the memory was uncomfortable.

'I thought you hated your job?' I said.

'I did, and I hardly spent any time in the office. I relied completely on the staff in my department who did all the work, but every now and then I'd put in a token appearance.

'Then one day one of the junior account managers came to me. He'd stumbled across some discrepancies in the figures, and when his managers had blown him off, he decided to approach me instead. I didn't know what I was looking at, but when he explained that one of my many cousins was dipping his fingers into the hedge funds I thought I'd better do something about it.' George laughed shortly. 'Big mistake, as it turned out.'

I frowned. 'But wasn't it your job to do something?'

'I thought so,' he said. 'The truth was that I didn't have a clue what I was doing, so I went to see my father and my uncle and explained the situation to them. They told me not to worry about it. They'd deal with it, they said. And they dealt with it by sacking the junior account manager who'd brought it to my attention in the first place.'

I was so shocked that I could only gape at him. 'They did *what*?'

'They fired him.' George's voice was quiet, implacable, and I realised that he was still very angry.

'What did you do?'

'I went back to them and told them that was unaccept-able. They'd chosen to protect family at the expense of a member of staff with real integrity. We had a huge row, during which it was pointed out—correctly—that I'd spent my whole life sponging off the company and that I only had the job because I was a member of the family and they didn't know what else to do with me. Also that I was too stupid to understand the fine details.'

I realised that my hands were clenched into fists, and I made myself relax them. There was nothing stupid about George, as his family would have known if they'd ever bothered to talk to him instead of dismissing him. I wasn't surprised that he had opted for a dissolute lifestyle. When his own family thought of him as a waste of space, what incentive had there been for him to apply himself?

'I got the message,' George said. 'I didn't know what I was talking about, and I was to shut up and stop making trouble.'

'You could have done that,' I said. 'You could have believed them, but you didn't.'

'No,' he said, remembering. 'I was so angry, I went straight out and called the Serious Fraud Office, and then it all hit the proverbial fan.'

'It must have been awful.' No matter how fraught my relationship with my father, I knew I would have found it difficult to denounce him to the authorities.

'You know, if they'd taken my cousin and dealt with him quietly, I wouldn't have minded,' George said, sounding weary, 'but the fact that they sacked Peter for being a troublemaker when he was just trying to do his job…I saw red.'

'I'm not surprised,' I said. I did have a vague memory of a whistle-blowing scandal a few years earlier, but I had just graduated and was getting used to my first job and thinking about getting chartered. I hadn't had much interest in business news.

'I didn't set out to single-handedly ruin the name of the family firm,' George said. 'It's not as if I had anything to be proud about, but I couldn't stand by and let Peter take the blame.'

'How did the rest of your family react?' I asked curiously. Surely *someone* had recognised that he was doing the decent thing?

'They closed ranks. Challoners are like that.' George smiled without humour. 'It's a family tradition. I came under a lot of pressure to withdraw the allegations. It all got very nasty.'

'So they fired you for doing the right thing?'

He shrugged. 'For my family, dragging the family name into disrepute is the worst thing you could possibly do.'

'But didn't anyone take your side? Your mother?'

'My mother?' George gave a mirthless laugh. 'My mother's even more obsessed with the family name than my father is—and that's saying something! She was never what you'd call a maternal type. I think she thought about her children as her contribution to the dynasty, and once she'd had Harry and me as the heir and spare she felt she'd done her duty.'

'That's awful,' I said, appalled.

'Oh, she wasn't cruel, neither of them were,' he said. 'They just weren't very interested in us. We had nannies and then we were sent away to school until we could join Challoners. And it's not as if we were deprived. We had everything we could ever want.'

'I'm not surprised you're so close to your grandmother,' I said. 'It sounds as if she was the only one who ever gave you any attention.'

His voice softened. 'Yes, Harry and I used to live for the holidays we spent with Letitia. We had some good times there.'

'Couldn't Harry have stood by you? He's your brother, after all!'

George didn't answer immediately. 'Harry was married with two children,' he said, and I had the impression he was picking his words with care. 'He couldn't afford to give up a house and a job and everything that goes along with toeing the line at Challoners.'

'*You* gave it all up.'

'I didn't have anyone depending on me. I don't blame Harry,' said George. 'He had to think of the kids.'

He didn't blame Harry, he didn't blame his mother, he didn't blame his fiancée. I sat on the stone step beside George, and felt chastened when I remembered how often I had blamed my father for everything that had gone wrong.

I should take a lesson from George. My chest hurt when I thought about what it must have been like for him then. Ostracised by his family, rejected by his fiancée, abandoned by his brother, dropped by his friends... Anyone else would be bitter and miserable, but not George. That laid-back manner, that carefree charm, hid more courage than I had ever imagined.

I wanted to rant and rail about his horrible family, but instead I leant my shoulder against his. 'I'm sorry, George,' I said quietly. 'You must have been so lonely.'

'I've got to admit I've had better times. They all said I'd never cope left to my own devices, and it was a fair assumption. After all, I'd had everything handed to me on a plate before. Suddenly I found myself without all the things I'd taken for granted before: no money, no job, nowhere to live. Even my car was provided by Challoners. It's not surprising Annabel wanted out,' he said. 'And my chances of finding a job were pretty slim once the word was out that I was a whistle-blower and couldn't be trusted to play by the rules—a lot of doors were slammed closed on me. My family have a lot of connections,' he added with a grim smile.

'Couldn't you have gone to your grandmother?'

'I could have done, yes, but I didn't want to involve her in a family row. Besides, once they all told me I'd never manage on my own, I was determined to prove them wrong. And, in the end, it was the best possible thing that could have happened to me.

'I'm happy now,' he said, and his arm lifted to gather me into his side. Turning his head, he smiled down into my face. 'Right this moment, I couldn't be happier, in fact.'

CHAPTER EIGHT

THE air leaked out of my lungs as I looked up at him. My heart was jerking madly, my pulse thundering in anticipation, and every cell in my body strained to lean into him.

So I let them.

'I'm happy too,' I said. 'Right this moment.'

I had forgotten my earlier doubts. George wasn't Charles. He was a decent man who had done the right thing. He had admitted his mistakes and had the courage to change. Why had I resisted him for so long?

'George,' I said, 'do you remember that night in your cottage when we kissed?'

He cast his eyes up and pretended to think. 'Now let me see, would that be the kiss I've only thought about every minute of every day since then?'

'I thought you'd forgotten,' I said involuntarily and he laughed and tightened his arm around me.

'How could I forget a kiss like that?'

'But you were so...normal!'

'I knew that if I wasn't, you'd freeze me out,' he said. 'I didn't want that.'

'I lost my nerve,' I confessed.

It was easier to talk in the dark, easier to talk side by side without those bright eyes on my face. 'The thing is, you were probably right about me being screwed up about my father,' I said. 'I don't find it easy to let go.' I swallowed. 'I'm afraid of losing control. It makes me feel the way I did when my mother died, and I hate it.'

George ran a finger down my cheek, and the tenderness of the gesture stopped the breath in my throat. 'I do understand, Frith.'

'When we kissed, it was so…so amazing.' I struggled to explain how I had felt that night. 'It was stronger than me, and I suppose I panicked. I thought the easiest thing would be to try and forget all about it, but I couldn't do it. I've been thinking about it ever since,' I told George. 'I've been wishing I wasn't such a coward, and wondering how to tell you that I'd changed my mind.'

'Did you think about saying: George, I've changed my mind?' said George, a smile in his voice.

'It didn't seem that easy,' I said. 'And then I decided it was probably all for the best. I was afraid you might be disappointed in me, and then we couldn't be friends any more.'

'*Disappointed*?' His arm fell from round me and he stared incredulously at me.

At least the darkness hid my flush. 'I'm not very experienced,' I said with difficulty. 'I'm not exciting and fun like your other girlfriends.'

'How do you know what my other girlfriends were like?'

'You said that Annabel was sexy and fun,' I reminded him with a trace of sulkiness. 'I just assumed they were all like her.'

George was shaking his head. 'Frith Taylor, you have the self-confidence of a slug,' he told me sternly. 'Between them, Charles and your father have a lot to answer for.' He smoothed my hair away from my face. 'You're exciting just sitting here, Frith.'

'Really?' My heart lifted with hope.

'Really,' he said gravely. 'But now I've changed my mind.'

George's smile deepened at what must have been my look of dismay. 'Maybe I *could* be happier...' He cupped my cheek with his hand and we leant in to each other at the same time, and when our lips met I let out a little sigh of thankfulness that I could kiss him at last, the way I'd been thinking about doing all month.

He tasted so good, he felt so good. I gasped as his fingers slid around and tangled in my hair, holding me to him, snarling up my senses until I couldn't tell touch from taste, couldn't tell if I was hearing his soft murmurs or feeling them drift enticingly over my ears. Was that the crisp smell of his shirt beneath my palms, the taste of his lip searing my skin?

Time stretched and swirled, while the summer night wrapped itself around us and the sweetness swirled higher and higher. Gasping with need, I pressed into George's unyielding body, and let his hands unlock my last defences.

'Frith?' he said raggedly, blizzarding kisses down my throat, and I arched into him with a shudder of pleasure.

'Yes?'

'Tell me you're ready to forget your plan for tonight?'

Forget the plan? This was what I had wanted, but still I felt as if I were on the edge of that abyss, looking down from a dizzying height and wondering if I dared to leap out into the air, wondering if I could trust George to catch me or if I would fall as if I had fallen before.

'The plan's still there,' I said, running my hand over his shoulder, wanting to make sure he understood. 'I'm not going to give it up completely. But that's for later. I don't have a plan for tonight.'

George got to his feet and reached down a hand to help me up. 'I do,' he said.

We never got round to closing the curtains. I was woken early the next morning by a stripe of sunlight across my pillow. I stirred and rolled away from it, and found my face pressed against George's warm shoulder. Mumbling something, he turned over, and left me to contemplate his broad, smoothly muscled back.

What had I done?

Heat stole through me as I remembered *exactly* what I had done. My body was still thrumming with pleasure, but my mind was now on full alert and it was no time at all before all those insecurities I'd turned away the night before started crowding in again.

Had I been exciting enough for George? What if he had just been amusing himself all along? Last night might have been wonderful, but what would he think when he saw my unimpressive breasts and my round tummy and my very ordinary legs in the cold light of day? What if he took one look and rolled away in disgust?

And even if he didn't, how was I going to concentrate on my job now, always wondering if he was going to appear, wondering if we would make love again? It would be even harder if I knew we *were* going to make love. How on earth could I focus on budgets and building schedules and drainage systems when I'd be thinking about the night to come, about his hard hands and his mouth and his strong, sleek body?

This was *exactly* why I hadn't wanted to get involved before! I reminded myself, far too late. My previous boyfriends had never cost me a moment's distraction from the job.

I needed to think about applying for a job overseas, too. Hugh would be coming back to work before too long, then what would I do? I couldn't hang around Whellerby, waiting for George to get tired of me, as he surely would. Last night might have been heart-stopping for me, but why should it have been anything special for George? He was so obviously an experienced lover and I was...I was just ordinary, in that as in so much else.

I gazed at his back, my hands twitching with the need to lay my palm against it for reassurance, to slide it down his flank and feel the sleek warmth of his skin. I wanted nothing more than to burrow into him and forget my career, forget my independence, forget everything but the spiral-ling pleasure of touching and being touched.

But that was exactly what I shouldn't do. That was the mistake my mother had made. She had learned her lesson when my father left us, and I had learned mine when she died. It was dangerous to rely on anyone else for your hap-piness. You had to make your own life and be independent. A career would never let you down.

That was why I had worked so hard to get qualified. That was why I had a plan, and why I should stick with it. My plan might not be fun or spontaneous or exciting, and the thought of it might not make my bones melt with an-ticipation, but it was safe.

My plan meant saying goodbye to George, sooner or later, and it was only now that I realised just how hard that was going to be.

Without turning, George reached an arm behind him and patted my hip. 'Stop fretting,' he said.

'I'm not fretting,' I said fretfully.

'Yes, you are.' He rolled over to face me, and my heart

turned over at the sight of him, rumpled and smiling and lazily satisfied. In the early morning light, his eyes were a deep, warm blue. 'I can feel you vibrating away like a tuning fork. You're supposed to be relaxed, and instead you're making the whole mattress jiggle with tension,' he said, and then went into a whole thing where he pretended the bed was shaking with it, throwing himself around and going completely over the top as usual.

'I'm not that bad!' I protested, laughing in spite of myself. 'It's just—'

George stopped me by laying his fingers against my mouth. 'It's just that it's the weekend,' he finished for me. 'It's just that the sun is shining and it's going to be a lovely day. It's just that we're naked together in a comfortable bed, and the one thing we don't need to worry about is feeling awkward because it wasn't very good between us last night.'

He kissed me then, a long, lazy kiss that left me boneless with pleasure and then lifted his head to look down into my face with those eyes that saw a little too much for comfort. 'Please tell me you're not worrying about that!'

'No,' I promised him, not entirely truthfully. I was worrying instead about it being *too* good. I was worrying about how I was going to miss him when I left. 'I'm not, really I'm not.'

I must have been a better liar than I thought because he smiled, and my heart swelled.

'Good,' he said, 'because it's too nice a day to be worrying about anything.' He lowered his head until his mouth brushed mine. 'I think we should find something else to do instead. What could we possibly do to stop you fretting?'

How could I fret when his warm weight was pressing on me, and the friction of skin against skin was making every nerve ending jump and spark? Throwing up its hands in defeat, my mind let my body take over, and sank unno-

ticed beneath a surge of need. I would think later. I hooked
my leg over George's, slid my arms around his neck and
pulled him closer.

'I'm sure we can think of something,' I said.

'Ready?' I slotted the key into the ignition and turned to
George in the passenger seat. He was all hunched up, like
a grown-up in a child's toy car.

'Don't you need to wind up the rubber bands in the engine first?' he said.

'There's no call to be rude about Audrey,' I said cheerfully, adjusting the rear-view mirror. 'At least she starts.'

It had been a sweet moment when George had turned up
the evening before, his usually good-humoured expression
darkened with a scowl. The alternator on the Land Rover
had gone, and if we were going to get to his grandmother's
birthday party Audrey was our best hope.

Only he didn't call her Audrey. He called her 'that heap
of scrap metal sitting outside your cottage'.

I was secretly nervous in case Audrey didn't, in fact,
start, but for once she obliged, and I settled back into the
driving seat trying not to show how relieved I was. I didn't
crow too much, though. I knew George was tense about
seeing his family again.

'I can't believe I'm going to turn up to Letitia's in a car
with eyelashes,' he grumbled as we rattled down the lane.

'Think of it as being lucky if you turn up at all,' I said,
mentally crossing my fingers that Audrey would survive
the long drive south. She was fine for little country lanes,
but even I couldn't claim that she was a good car for a motorway. I just hoped that she would get us there.

'What did you decide to get your grandmother as a present in the end?' I asked, changing the subject. We had been

throwing ideas around for the past six weeks with George unable to make a decision one way or another.

'You mean, apart from you?'

'I hope you're not thinking of tying a bow around my neck?' I said and was glad to see George grin.

'Now, that's an image I'd like to hold onto!' He shifted around to try and make himself comfortable in the old bucket seat. 'I found an old photo of me with Mabel,' he said, answering my original question. 'I've put it in a frame. It's not much, but I think it'll mean something to her.'

'That's a great idea!' I said, impressed.

'I hope she'll like it.' He slanted a look at me as I held primly onto the steering wheel and kept my eyes on the road. 'Maybe we could keep the idea of you with nothing but a ribbon round your neck for *my* birthday.'

I fought a smile. 'When is it?'

'October.'

My smile faded. 'I don't think I'll be here then.'

'What?'

'I'm sure Hugh will be better soon,' I said brightly. 'I've already started applying for other jobs, in fact.'

When I checked the mirror, I just caught his brows snapping together. 'What other jobs?'

'I told you,' I reminded him. 'The next step in my plan is to work on a major construction. I had a reply from the consultants on the new Shofrar airport just yesterday, in fact. They said to get in touch again when I was free to move out there, so that was good news.'

I had spent most of the night before trying to convince myself that it was good, anyway.

When my mind had returned that lovely, lazy Sunday, I had come to a decision. I was going to stick with my plan— no question about that—but while I was in Whellerby, which was, after all, part of the plan, there was no reason I shouldn't make the most of my time there.

As long as I didn't lose my head completely, as long as I kept the boundaries clear and didn't get too involved, it would be fine. Or so I told myself. But that first night with George had turned into the weekend, and the weekend into a week, and the more time passed, the harder it was to remember that I would be leaving.

The day I found myself drifting off in the middle of a technical discussion with Frank, I knew I had to get a grip. I was supposed to be thinking about reinforced steel joists, and instead my mind was on George and how he could make me gasp with pleasure one minute and laugh the next. I think I must have had a slack, silly smile on my face, because I caught Frank looking at me strangely. Mortified at having been caught behaving in such an unprofessional way, I went straight home that night and started applying for jobs.

Step two on my plan.

'When were you going to tell me?' George's voice held an edge I hadn't heard before.

'You always knew I was going to be moving on,' I told him, rather proud of my cool. 'I thought you'd be pleased, actually.'

'Pleased? How do you work that out?'

'Come on, George, you know I'm not the right woman for you,' I said. 'You want someone sweet and gentle who'll make scones and wear a pinny and be in the kitchen when you get home at night. And in case you hadn't noticed, that's not me.'

He swivelled round in his seat to stare at me. 'I never said that.'

'That was what you meant. You want a country girl, like your grandmother.'

George gave a crack of laughter. 'I never said Letitia was sweet!'

'You know what I mean,' I said, cross that he was making me spell it out. 'The fact is that we want completely different things. You want dogs and horses and living in the country, and I want a career. That's what I've planned.'

'Oh, yes, the Frith Taylor Plan for Life! How could I have forgotten?'

'I haven't forgotten,' I said evenly. 'I learnt a long time ago not to depend on anyone else for my happiness, George. It's too risky. Much better to concentrate on a job. At least with my career I have control. When you build a structure, you start with an idea, and then make a design, and then you put it together and make something real. That's a plan. Emotions don't work like that,' I said. 'You can't predict what people are going to do or what they're going to feel.'

'That's for sure,' said George sarcastically.

I didn't really understand why he was being so surly. 'You knew I felt like this,' I said. 'You knew I didn't want to get involved.'

'I knew you were *afraid* of getting involved.'

'Maybe that does make me a coward, but it's better than throwing up everything for something as unpredictable as a relationship. I don't want to let go. I don't want to end up lonely and bitter and sad like my mother.'

'You let go with me,' said George.

I coloured. 'In bed.'

'It's a place to start.'

'And I can do it because I know you don't really want someone like me,' I tried to explain. 'Because you've always known I'll be leaving—or I thought you knew.'

'I did know.' George let out a sigh. 'I just let myself forget.'

'It's been easy to forget,' I said, thinking of the past six weeks. 'We've had a lovely time, but nothing's changed really, has it? I still want a career overseas, and you still want to stay at Whellerby and build up the stables there. There's no way to compromise there.'

'You're right,' said George. 'We're doomed.'

I was glad to hear the smile back in his voice. 'It doesn't mean that we can't carry on having a good time until I go, though, does it?'

'No,' he agreed. 'Although I'm not sure this weekend is really going to count as a good time.'

'Are you nervous?' I asked, glancing at him. He was putting on a good show of unconcern but I knew that he had to be dreading the meeting to come.

'I can contain my excitement at the prospect,' said George. 'But this is for Letitia, and in twenty-four hours it will all be over.'

'Do you know who else is going to be there?'

'Just Letitia's immediate family, that is my father and my uncle, with wives obviously. And Harry.'

George's voice changed when he said his brother's name. He didn't talk much about Harry, but I had a feeling he was the one George missed most.

'He's married too, isn't he?'

'Yes, Charlotte will be there, and the boys.' His expression softened. 'They're great kids. Two boys, just like Harry and I were.'

'What about your cousin? The one who was embezzling the hedge funds?'

'Giles. Apparently he's on some work trip that couldn't be cancelled,' George said dryly.

'Well, that's something.' I had doubted my ability to keep a civil tongue in my head if I'd had to meet the man who had let George take the fall for him. 'What happened to him?'

'Oh, he would have had fingers rapped, but he hadn't done the unforgivable. He hadn't broken ranks, and he hadn't involved outsiders. He's still there, in fact. I feel fairly sure he'll be Chairman in a few years.' George smiled but without much humour. 'Old Giles knows how to play by the rules, and for the Challoners, as you know, the rules are everything.'

Audrey rattled her way down the motorway. She wasn't the fastest of cars, and it took us nearly five hours to get to Letitia Challoner's Wiltshire manor house.

It was dull driving along motorways, but I didn't want the journey to end. I like travelling. It's the only time I put plans on hold. Once you get into a car or a plane, there's nothing more you can do. There are no decisions to be made, no mistakes to be fretted over. I was committed to the pretence with George and now we were on our way, all we could do was to go on to the end and think about things when we got there.

Usually I prefer to travel on my own—and, yes, I get the symbolism—but I had to admit that the journey went quicker with George by my side. We squabbled over what music to listen to, whether a bacon sandwich should be made with brown sauce or ketchup and whether it was all right for drivers to sit in the middle lane when there are no cars in the slow lane—answer: no, whatever George says about me being a tense driver. Important stuff like that.

I was trying to distract George, and I did pretty well until we turned off the motorway at last, and he grew quieter. He directed me down roads that got narrower and narrower until we wound our way to a pretty village tucked away in the fold of the Wiltshire downs.

'There,' he said, pointing, and I drove Audrey through a pair of stone gates to stop in front of an old manor house.

Unlike Whellerby Hall, this house looked as if it had grown out of the ground, and the mellow stone glowed in the June sunshine.

A Bentley and a gleaming Rolls Royce were parked outside the house next to a top-of-the-range four-wheel drive, the kind that costs the price of a small house in some areas. The rest of the family were already here.

The gravel crunched beneath Audrey's wheels as I drew up beside their cars. I loved Audrey, but even I could see that she looked ridiculous with her battered lime-green paint and eyelashes. Another place I was obviously not going to fit in, I thought, and told myself I didn't care. Audrey might not be the most stylish car in the world, but at least she had got us there.

I turned off the engine and the silence fell around us like a stifling blanket. It was a perfect June day and the sun beat down on the metal roof. I'd been wearing sunglasses to drive, and I took them off and folded them carefully and put them in their case.

George drew a deep breath and let it out very slowly. Impulsively I leant over and put my hand on his thigh,

'It'll be fine,' I said.

George's hand closed over mine and he squeezed it wordlessly. 'I'm glad you're here,' he confessed.

I opened my mouth to say that I would always be there for him, but closed it with a snap before the words could come out. I wouldn't always be there, would I?

I got out of the car instead. No one had come rushing out to greet us. Not that I expected that. I'd always had to negotiate a bevy of assistants before being admitted to see my father. The idea that he would be waiting anxiously to see me, that he would throw open the door and welcome me in with a hug, was laughable.

'Do we knock, or what?' I said, looking doubtfully at the heavy front door.

'They'll be round the back,' said George, and he took my hand. 'We'll go that way.'

The house seemed to be drowsing in the sunshine. Old roses nodded around the windows and the air smelt of cut grass. The grounds were beautifully kept, with a cluster of stone outbuildings to one side and gardens stretching down to a railed paddock on the other. The trees were the fresh green of an early English summer, and I could hear wood pigeons burbling on the roof.

It should have been perfect, but I was too nervous about the meeting to come to appreciate how lovely it was. Not on my own account. It didn't matter to me if none of his family liked me—it wasn't as if I were ever going to meet them again—but I minded desperately that it wasn't too hard for George.

He was silent as he led me around the corner of the house to an immaculate lawn. I could see a group of people clustered on a terrace outside French windows that had been thrown open to the sun, and as we headed across the grass they stopped talking one by one and turned to watch us. Nobody said a thing.

I looked at George. At first glance he seemed as relaxed as ever, but I could see a muscle jumping in his jaw and feel the tension in the grip of his fingers. I plastered a smile on my own face as if I were anticipating a warm welcome.

There was a moment of utter stillness, then two boys leapt down the steps from the terrace and came tumbling across the lawn. 'Uncle George! Uncle George!' Clearly they hadn't been told about the family rift.

'Hey!' George spread his arms and scooped up the first to reach him, swung him round and turned him upside down to yells of laughter. The next boy leapt at him and all three of them went down in a pile.

Laughing, I glanced from them to the frozen group on the terrace. A man so like George that he had to be his brother Harry was staring at the boys scrambling excitedly over their uncle, his face stricken.

George extricated himself eventually and hauled the two boys to their feet. 'Meet my nephews,' he said, grinning, and I was relieved to see that the tension had broken. 'Completely wild, of course. Jack, Jeremy, this is Frith.'

'Hello,' I said.

They returned my greeting politely, but it was obvious that their attention was on their uncle. I didn't mind. I was pleased they were so obviously thrilled to see George. They were sturdy boys of about nine and eleven, I judged, with open faces and the blue Challoner eyes.

'We didn't know you were coming,' they told George.

His smile twisted a little. 'I guess they were keeping me as a great surprise.'

An arm around each of the boys' shoulders, he headed over to the bottom of the steps.

Nobody on the terrace had moved. They just stood and watched in utter silence. As we got closer I saw that they were clustered around an elderly lady who was sitting in a wicker chair, a stick propped against it. Letitia Challoner was frail but still formidable. I thought she looked as haughty as the sons who stood on either side of her, glaring at George, and I wondered why he was so fond of her.

George stopped at the bottom of the steps and smiled at his grandmother.

'Hello, Letitia,' he said. 'Happy birthday.'

'You're late,' she said.

'We left at the crack of dawn, I promise you,' he said

easily. 'Sadly Frith's car, while, er, characterful, isn't the fastest on the road. But we're here now.'

'I'm glad,' she said, and then she smiled and her whole face lit up. 'Come here, boy, and give me a kiss,' she said, beckoning him forward, and, without a glance at the rest of his family standing silently by, George let go of the boys and went up the steps to kiss her cheek.

'It's good to see you, Letitia.'

'It's been too long,' she said astringently, but her frail hand touched his hair in a gesture so full of love that my throat tightened.

'I know,' said George. 'I'm sorry.'

Straightening, he looked at the watching group. 'Hello, Mother,' he said, unsmiling. She had a hand to her throat and was staring at him in shock. 'Dad.'

The beefy-faced man on Letitia's other side was obviously his uncle. 'Andrew,' George acknowledged him. 'And Penny.' He smiled at Andrew's wife, whose gaze darted anxiously between him and her husband, obviously dreading the explosion that was to come.

'You've got a damned cheek coming here!' Andrew burst out. 'Who asked you to come?'

'I did,' said Letitia clearly. 'George is my grandson, and I wanted him here with me.'

Michael Challoner was a good-looking man like his son, but his eyes were hard. 'You should have told us he was coming.'

'And have you make a fuss? I'm tired of this nonsense about George letting you all down. He's family and I want you all to treat him that way this weekend. This is my house, and my party, and you're all to behave.'

Letitia Challoner might be old, but she still had the whip hand. Her sons exchanged a glance, but they weren't prepared to argue with her.

George's gaze had moved on to his brother. 'Hello, Harry,' he said quietly.

Harry had the same dark gold hair, the same features, the same lean build, but he wasn't the same at all. Next to George, he was somehow muted. There was no laughter dancing in his eyes, no smile tugging at his mouth. When I looked at him, my pulse didn't kick, and my bones didn't dissolve with longing.

I thought I saw yearning in Harry's eyes in place of laughter. George had told me how close the two brothers had been as boys. Harry must have remembered that too as he watched his own sons throw themselves at their uncle. For a moment it seemed as if he would step forward and hug his brother, but he caught his father's eye and in the end he just nodded back.

'George.'

There was an uncomfortable silence.

'And who's this?' Letitia swung her gaze to me waiting awkwardly at the bottom of the steps. George had inherited his blue eyes from his grandmother. Hers might be faded with age, but they were still sharp.

'This is Frith.' George held out a hand, and I climbed the steps, burningly aware of everyone's eyes on me. They were all smartly dressed, ready for the celebratory lunch, and I felt scruffy in the jeans and white T-shirt I'd worn for driving.

'You told me to find myself a sensible girl, and I have,' George told his grandmother and she looked me up and down, clearly reserving judgement.

'Humph. *I'll* decide if she's sensible or not.'

Letitia might be ninety, but this was no dotty old lady. She was sharp as tacks, and she would pick up any false note. I couldn't bear the thought of her calling George on the pretence. It would be just an added humiliation for him in front of his family. If Letitia realised that we weren't really in love, it wouldn't be my fault, I decided.

'Happy birthday, Mrs Challoner,' I said, letting go of George's hand to shake hers.

'What sort of gal takes up with my grandson?'

'One who loves him very much,' I said with a smile at George, who smiled back, an arrested expression in the blue, blue eyes.

'Well, that's not very sensible for a start.' Andrew Challoner snorted in the background, but we ignored him.

'Frith's a civil engineer,' George told his grandmother.

'Unusual.' Letitia inspected my face more carefully. 'Do you ride, Frith?'

'Only a bicycle, I'm afraid.'

CHAPTER NINE

'I THOUGHT my lack of horse-riding experience was going to count against me,' I whispered to George when the house-keeper showed us to our room to change before lunch. By the time Letitia had finished cross-examining me, it was getting late, and the meal had already been set back an hour. The cook would be cursing me, I thought.

'She liked you, I could tell.' Careless of the fact that they were waiting for us downstairs, George kicked off his shoes and threw himself down on the bed. In chinos and a pale yellow polo shirt, he looked wonderful, and I wished that we were in a hotel, that there were no family to be faced, no formal lunch to be eaten.

In a hotel, I could go over to the bed and sit next to him. I could push my hair out of the way and lean down to press my lips to his throat. I could kiss my way up to the pulse that beat below his ear, to the jaw that made me weak with desire whenever I looked at it. I could tug the shirt from his trousers and slide my hand beneath it. I could explore the broad solid chest, let my mouth drift over the sleek warmth of his skin.

But we weren't in a hotel. We were late for lunch.

I turned away, swallowing, and opened my case.

'It's better to be honest, anyway,' George was saying,

unaware—I hoped!—of the lustful turn of my thoughts. 'She can pick up a fib a mile off.'

I made a big thing of shaking out my dress. 'I told her I loved you,' I objected.

'So you did.' The dent in his cheek deepened with his lopsided smile as he got up from the bed. Grabbing his shirt below the collar, he hauled it over his head, the way men did. 'Maybe you do love me,' he said, muffled.

My mouth dried at the sight of his lean, hard body, already so achingly familiar. If only we could forget the lunch and his icily polite family, and spend the afternoon in that wide, inviting bed with the afternoon sunshine spilling through the open window.

'Maybe she can't spot a pretence quite as well as you think she can,' I said, unsettled by how badly I wanted to touch him. This wasn't like me. There was a time and a place for lazy afternoons in bed, and the middle of a fraught family reunion wasn't one of them.

Anyone would think I couldn't keep my hands off George. I was going to have to get used to not being able to touch him sooner or later, and I'd better start now.

'Maybe I'm a better actor than you think I am,' I added, hoping that it was true. Because if it wasn't true, I was in trouble.

Big trouble.

No, it wasn't love I felt, I reassured myself. Lust, maybe, but I had been so careful not to think beyond these few weeks. I had my emotions well under control as always. My relationship with George was firmly time-limited, like all the best plans, and I hadn't forgotten that. Hadn't we just been discussing that in the car? I would be leaving soon. There was no point in doing anything silly like falling in love with him.

Of course I wasn't going to do that.

George had been vague when I asked him how formal the lunch was likely to be, so I had played safe and brought my favourite summer dress. With its soft chintzy print, it was faintly old-fashioned, but I'd always liked it. It had a chiffon overskirt that floated when I walked, and it made me feel pretty.

It wasn't the most exciting dress in the world, but I felt comfortable in it, and, with some heels and my mother's pearls around my throat, I was ready to go.

George stared at me as he shrugged on his jacket. In spite of the heat, the men were all wearing suits. 'You look gorgeous,' he said. 'You should wear a dress more often.'

'I don't think this would be very practical on site,' I said briskly to hide my pleasure.

'Who cares about the site? You could wear it for me.'

I touched the pearls at my throat. They reminded me of my mother. She had done everything my father asked of her. If he'd wanted her to wear a bin bag, she'd have done it to please him, and look where it had got her. I didn't need to please George, I reminded myself.

'I'll wear what I feel like,' I said.

In deference to Letitia's age, the lunch was the main celebration of the day. We had champagne, and then a whole salmon with hollandaise sauce and tiny new potatoes boiled and tossed in parsley.

I would have enjoyed it if it hadn't been for the undercurrent of tension running around the table. Everyone was on their best behaviour, but there was still an edge to the conversation, a stiltedness to the way the family talked to each other. Margaret and Michael Challoner didn't address George directly once, but I saw them looking at him with a kind of baffled frustration, as if they couldn't understand what had gone wrong.

It was hard to believe George was their son. I wondered if he had always been regarded as the cuckoo in the nest. It would certainly explain why he had kicked out against the stultifying formality of the family.

At least he had forged a strong bond with his grandmother. I watched them together, and it was obvious that George was Letitia's favourite. He teased her and made her laugh and if he was aware of his parents' coldness, he gave no sign of it. It was left to me to make laboured conversation with them and with George's uncle and aunt. They were too well bred to be overtly rude to me, but I could tell that they weren't impressed.

I didn't care. The feeling was mutual. Charlotte made little effort. She was one of those pale, wilting women with wills of iron.

The only decent conversation I had was with the two boys, Jack and Jeremy. They were a little subdued by the atmosphere but happy to talk about some computer game they liked to play. I didn't really follow the details, but I gathered it was set on some alien planet populated by hideous monsters and we had an interesting discussion about space travel and the likelihood of life on Mars.

They were nice boys. I'd never had much to do with children before, and I was surprised at how easy they were to talk to. Long ago I had decided against having children of my own. Children needed too much, and how could you ever guarantee that they would be happy? That you would always be there for them? That a blood clot wouldn't strike you down just when they needed you most? I couldn't bear the thought of letting a child down, the way my father had let me down, or of leaving him or her alone.

Still, chatting to Jeremy and Jack made me think that having a family might be fun too. I wondered what it would be like to be a normal family—like the ones you saw in the TV adverts anyway—and sit happily around a table, talking together. I even indulged myself in a little dream where I was at one end of the table, a couple of blue-eyed kids in the middle, and their father at the other end, gazing fondly at me and our children...

Only then I realised that the man across the table from me was George, and I yanked the fantasy firmly to a halt before it could go any further. George wasn't for me. Children weren't for me. There was no point in a dream like that.

At least it got me through the lunch.

It was a relief when Letitia announced that she was tired and going to rest. 'Come on, Frith,' said George the moment the door closed behind her. 'Let's go for a walk. I'll show you where Harry and I used to get into mischief.'

The boys leapt up, obviously as eager to escape from the frigid atmosphere as George and I were. 'Can we come?'

'Of course.' George looked at his brother. 'Harry?'

Harry's gaze flicked between his wife and his parents, who looked stonily back at him. He hesitated, then pushed back his chair with a kind of defiance. 'Why not?'

I'd had hopes that George and I might get to spend the afternoon in the sunny bedroom after all, but I was glad later that we'd gone out. I changed back into my jeans, and then George led the way out into the summer afternoon, Jack and Jeremy leaping on either side of him like puppies.

I followed more slowly with Harry. 'I didn't realise George would be so good with kids,' I said.

Harry smiled. He was more relaxed out here away from the rest of the family. I was afraid Charlotte would have wanted to come too, but she had gone to rest too. Apparently it was exhausting driving an hour from London and having to look after your own children for a whole morning.

'The boys always loved George. He's more fun than anyone else and he never talked down to them.' Harry glanced at me. 'He'd be a great father.'

He would. I could imagine him playing with his sons, blue-eyed, tousle-haired boys just like him, or swinging a daughter up so that she could ride on his shoulders. He would love them and make them laugh and keep them safe.

Something twisted inside me at the thought of George with children of his own. At the thought that they wouldn't be my children. It made my chest ache and to my horror I felt tears clog my throat. I *never* cried. Crying meant letting go and losing control and I wasn't about to start now, but I was very glad of the sunglasses that shaded my eyes.

'Yes, he would,' I said after a moment with a non-committal smile.

'Are you and George thinking…?'

'Oh, no.' I even managed a laugh. Not a very good one, but a definite laugh. 'We're not nearly there yet.'

'It's just you seem really good together,' said Harry. 'George needs someone like you.'

How little he knew his own brother! I was the last kind of girl George needed. Having met his mother, so coldly focused on the success of the bank, I could understand even more why George longed for the warmth and comfort of a true homemaker. I was never going to be one of those.

We poked around in the barns, stuck our heads up into the old apple loft and explored the stables, sadly empty now, and then we crossed the fields into the dappled shade of the little wood at the far side where a stream ran sluggishly. Clearly they hadn't had all the rain that had plagued my site in the early days.

The smell of wild garlic was intense in the heat of the afternoon. I pulled at the burrs that clung to my jeans. 'I can see what a great place this must have been for boys,'

I said. 'George told me about all the holidays you used to spend here together.'

'Yes, we had some good times.' Harry looked sad.

'He misses you, I think.'

Harry didn't answer at first. We were walking side by side along the edge of the stream. 'I should have supported him,' he said suddenly. 'But I had school fees to think about and Charlotte felt...' He trailed off. 'Well, anyway, I should have stuck by him. I knew he was doing the right thing.'

'George doesn't blame you, Harry.'

'I blame myself.' Harry's mouth set in a straight line, and suddenly he looked much more like George.

'It's hard for him, cut off from everyone,' I said tentatively. 'Maybe you could see each other every now and then?'

He nodded. 'I'll talk to Charlotte about it. Letitia's right. This rift has gone on long enough.'

I hoped that Harry would make the effort. It wasn't my business to interfere between George and his brother, but I hated the thought that George was going to be alone when I left.

Which was ridiculous, of course. George had masses of friends. He didn't need me. Still, I liked the idea that he could reconnect with his family. At least I had Saffron.

Ahead, George and the boys had stopped and were peering up into the branches of an old oak.

'I was just wondering if it's still there...yes, see that?' George pointed up to a straggle of frayed rope. 'Your father and I used to swing across this stream on that.'

'Until it broke,' said Harry. 'George fell in the water and broke his ankle the day we were due back at school.'

'Remember how we rigged up our own version of paintball in the wood?'

Harry laughed. 'And the trouble we got into when the

entire paint pot fell on that busybody neighbour of Letitia's when she was walking her yappy little dog?'

After that, they vied with each other for the memory of the times they had been at their naughtiest, and of course the two boys drank it in. It turned into a nice afternoon in the end. We found a bridge further upstream and played pooh sticks, and then we sat in the long grass and dangled our feet in the water.

On the way back, we stopped to talk to the ponies in the neighbouring paddocks. At least, George and the boys did. I hung back. I didn't care what George told me about holding my palm flat, I couldn't forget just what big teeth those horses had.

'Do you ride?' I asked Harry, who was watching his brother and his sons with a smile.

He shook his head. 'Not any more. George was always the one with the horses. He's absolutely brilliant with them. I'm glad he's got the chance to ride up in Yorkshire. George is never going to be happy without a horse.'

George needed more than a horse, I thought. After seeing him with his nephews, I thought he needed a family of his own too

A family he could never have with me.

That evening we gathered for drinks on the terrace. The heat of the afternoon had faded, and the shadows were just starting to stretch across the lawn in the golden light.

Letitia looked fabulous in a burgundy dress and jacket, a magnificent sapphire necklace around her neck and diamond rings winking on her gnarled fingers. The other women were similarly glamorous and bejewelled. I felt distinctly underdressed in my plain red wrap dress, in spite of recycling the pearls and heels I'd worn earlier.

Dinner was not a comfortable occasion. Letitia retired

after the toast, and the boys were also in bed, which left George's uncle, Andrew, to rule the roost.

I didn't care for Andrew. He was a bully, I decided, and Michael Challoner was spineless for not standing up to him in support of his son. We women did our best to keep a stilted conversation going, but Andrew was determined to make George pay for the family's wounded pride, and the moment there was a pause, he would start hectoring.

Every mistake George had ever made was flung out. Every exam he'd ever failed, every opportunity he'd ever squandered.

'All the money that was spent on your education,' Andrew ranted. 'Everything you ever had you owed to your family, and what did you do? Fling it back in our faces!'

George refused to rise to the bait, but he was holding himself under tight control, I could tell. When I put a hand on his back in wordless support, it was rigid beneath my palm. I tried to rub it comfortingly, but it was like trying to loosen up an iron bar.

'You've always been useless,' Andrew sneered. 'What good have you ever been to anybody?'

I took my hand from George's back. I had had enough.

'That's rubbish,' I said clearly. 'George has more integrity than anyone I know.'

'Leave it, Frith,' said George. 'It doesn't matter.'

'It *does* matter. Your family of all people should know what you're really like.'

'We *do* know what he's like! You don't know what you're talking about,' snarled Andrew. 'You're like every other silly girl, carried away by a pretty face, and, God knows, George has played on that over the years, haven't you, George?

'You want to be careful, missy,' he said to me when

George didn't respond. 'You're only the latest in a very long queue. If you think you can trust him, think again!'

I was getting angry by then. 'For a start, Mr Challoner, I am not a silly girl, I'm a chartered civil engineer. I've worked with a lot of men in the past few years, and there isn't a single one of them I'd trust more than George.'

'Pah! What do you know? Nobody else would trust him further than they could throw him now.'

'Horses do.'

'Horses?' Andrew exploded. 'Who cares about a bloody horse? I'm talking about people who matter. You wouldn't trust him if you knew what he did to this family's reputation in the City.'

'I do know what he did,' I said. 'He did the right thing. That's why I trust him, why everyone trusts him. The people who matter to me, anyway.

'The thing is that whenever George is around, you know things are going to be OK,' I said, raising my voice to talk over George, who was trying to tell me not to bother.

'The tenants at Whellerby like him, because if they need something done to their homes, George makes sure it gets done. He saw that Lord Whellerby needed to expand facilities on the estate, and he got the conference centre built. When my sister turned up out of the blue in a crisis, it was George who knew what had to be done and how to do it.'

I drew a breath. 'I don't want to hear anyone ever tell me that George is useless. He's the most useful man I know!'

There was silence around the table, then Harry said, 'Hear, hear!'

'Are you planning to disgrace the family too?' Andrew roared, and Charlotte flashed Harry an accusing look. 'If you want to keep your cushy little number, you'll—'

'I think that's enough,' Margaret Challoner broke in with a glacial look around the table that shut even Andrew up.

'I've already lost one son from the bank, and I don't wish to lose another. I think it's time we drew a line under the whole unfortunate incident.'

Unfortunate incident? I stared at her in disbelief. Her son had been fired and ostracised from the family for standing up for what was right and she thought it was *unfortunate*?

She wasn't exactly a tiger fighting for her cubs, but, as maternal went, it was probably the best Margaret could do. Anyway, it did the trick. Andrew subsided, George made an effort to talk about interest rates with his father, and I spent the rest of the meal encouraging Charlotte to talk about school fees and house prices and the difficulties of finding a decent au pair.

The only thing that made it bearable was George's warm hand on my thigh. He was feeling better, I guessed, especially when his fingers found the edge of my wrap dress, and slipped beneath it to my bare skin, tracing teasing patterns on my inner thigh until I squirmed in my chair.

I kept losing track of what Charlotte was saying. 'That's terrible,' I said when she told me about Jeremy's scholarship, and apparently I punctuated her distressed account of a light-fingered cleaner with 'mmm...yes...great... wonderful...'

It was only when I realised George was shaking with suppressed laughter that I snapped back to attention and pushed his hand hastily away. 'I'm so sorry, Charlotte,' I said penitently. 'I missed that. What were you saying?'

The moment everyone pushed back their chairs, I leapt to my feet, hastily pulling my skirt back into place around my knees and avoiding George's eyes. We practically ran up the stairs together, and started to laugh as we fell through the door.

'That was one of the worst evenings of my life,' I said as I leant back against the door, already weak-kneed with

anticipation. I might not be able to give George the family
he needed, but that night I was there for him.

'I'm sorry. I won't ever put you through that again, I
promise.'

George lifted his hand to stroke the hair back from my
face. His warm fingers lingered against my skin, drifting
tantalisingly down my throat, to the deep V of my dress.

'I've been thinking about doing this all evening,' he said.

My smile evaporated as his hands smoothed possessively
over my breasts. 'I wouldn't have got through it without
you,' said George, not quite evenly. 'Or without this dress.
Whenever Andrew started, I thought about how I was going
to unfasten it,' he said, his hands finding the tie.

Very slowly, he unknotted it with deft fingers and pulled
the dress open. 'I thought about how good it was going to
feel when I could do this,' he said, pushing the soft mate-
rial from my shoulders, and my breath grew choppy at the
look in his eyes.

'Anything to help,' I managed and he smiled.

'Well, now you come to mention it, there *is* one more
thing you could do to help me relax,' he said, securing my
waist with hard hands and pulling me towards him.

I went unresisting, boneless with desire. 'What's that?'
I whispered.

'I'll show you,' he said, and did.

The answer phone was blinking when we got back to the
cottage the next day. I pressed the play button as George
dumped the bags and opened the fridge in search of a beer,
and the message echoed into the kitchen.

'Frith? Hugh here.' Even through the static, Hugh
sounded stronger than I'd heard him in a long time. 'Just
to say that the doctors are telling me I can go back to work
in a month. I know you're keen to get out to Shofrar, so I

think I can persuade them that I'll be fine after three weeks.
Are you OK to stay until then? Isn't that about when your
sister's wedding is, anyway? Give me a ring when you get
this and we'll coordinate dates.'

George had stilled with his head bent towards the fridge,
and I was still standing by the phone when the message
ended with a beep, and the recorded voice started up. *To
hear this message again, press one. To save the message,
press—*

I clicked the machine off.

The fridge hummed into the silent kitchen. George
pulled out a beer and straightened as he closed the door.

'Good news,' he said.

'What?'

'About Hugh being better.'

'Oh, yes…yes, it is. It's great,' I said, but I was thinking: *A month. I'm going to have to say goodbye to George
in a month.* Panic fluttered in my stomach.

'You'd better get back to those people about the Shofrar
job,' said George, levering the top off the bottle, and the
sound of the air whooshing out seemed to fill the kitchen.

I swallowed, but it didn't get rid of the tightness in my
throat. 'I'll email them later.'

Another agonising pause, then George put down the beer
and came over to pull me against him. 'Hey, don't look like
that,' he said. 'We knew this wasn't going to last for ever,
didn't we?'

I nodded dumbly against his chest.

'You said that in the car.'

More dumb nodding. I had said that. I had meant it too.
Intellectually, I had always understood that being with
George was only ever going to be a temporary thing. I'd
told myself that. It was part of the deal I'd made with myself. I just hadn't understood how it would *feel.*

I put my arms around his waist and held onto him while I breathed in the clean, male, familiar smell that was just George and drew on his strength.

'It's much better to say goodbye when things are going well,' I tried. My face was pressed into his throat and my voice came out muffled.

'Exactly,' said George.

'I mean, you'd just get bored with me if I hung around too long.'

'Bound to,' he agreed.

I pulled away slightly to look up into his face. 'Do…do you think you could put up with me for another month?'

George pretended to consider. 'I could probably manage that,' he said.

'So, you'll still come to Saffron's wedding?'

'Of course I will!' he said, giving me an exasperated little shake. 'Nothing's going to change. We're going to make the most of the last month, we're going to have a good time, we're going to the wedding together, and then you're going to get yourself a great job in Shofrar, just like you planned.'

I hadn't planned for the coldness that sat like a stone in my belly whenever I thought about saying goodbye, but I told myself George was right. I needed to stick to my plan. It had never let me down before, and it wouldn't now.

So I sent that email and fixed up a job in Shofrar to start six weeks later. Not just a job, *exactly* the job I wanted on the new airport. I agreed with Hugh that he would take over the week before Saffron's wedding. I'd already promised Saffron I would spend that time with her, soothing her pre-wedding jitters like a good bridesmaid should. After the wedding, I would come back with George and pack up my stuff. We'd have a last week, and then I'd fly out to Shofrar, for step two of my plan.

Everything was working out perfectly. I should have been ecstatic.

I did a pretty good job of pretending that I was.

'Are you sure you're going to be all right?'

I left Audrey outside the cottage and George drove me to the station in York. I hated prolonged goodbyes, so I'd told him just to drop me off, but he stopped me as I had my hand on the door handle.

'I'll be fine,' I said lightly. 'It's a million pound wedding. What could possibly go wrong?'

'I was thinking about you seeing your father again.'

'Oh, that,' I said, my eyes sliding from his. I was dreading it, of course.

'I know how it feels,' he reminded me. 'You know how difficult it was for me to see my parents at Letitia's party.'

'And it was fine in the end, wasn't it?'

'Only because you were there. You're going to be on your own,' said George.

'I'm used to it,' I said, and put on a bright smile as I opened the door. 'See you for the rehearsal dinner, and don't be late!'

I *was* used to dealing with things on my own. It was easier that way, I reminded myself all the way to London, but I couldn't help wishing that George were with me after all as I knocked on the door of my father's lavish house in Knightsbridge.

There were a few paparazzi lurking outside, but they didn't bother to take pictures of me. I'm fairly sure they assumed that I was a secretary or some menial employee. I'd dressed carefully down in jeans and a white shirt and I carried my meagre wardrobe in a small overnight bag.

My heart was thundering in my throat as the butler let

me into the house. *Get it over with*, I told myself. 'Is my father in?'

Any normal daughter would able to go and find her father and throw herself into his arms. I had to wait rigidly while the butler spoke to my father's assistant, who spoke to his PA, who came out to the hall after a few minutes.

'Your father will see you now.'

I wondered if he had told them to make me cool my heels for a while, just to remind me who was in charge. It was the kind of thing he would do.

He was standing behind his desk, reading a document, but he looked at me over the top of half-moon glasses when I went in. I didn't remember him wearing glasses before. It had been six years since I stood there and asked him to come to my graduation. He was looking older, I thought, but still stocky, still with the same bullish expression and powerful presence that I had admired and resented at the same time for so long.

Dad put down the paper and came round the desk with a certain wariness.

'Frith,' he acknowledged me, his expression unreadable.

He made no move to kiss me, and I had a sudden, bitter memory of being a little girl, hopping with excitement when I heard him coming through the door. He used to crouch down and smile.

'Where's my girl?' he'd ask, and I would rush into his arms, squealing, 'I'm here, I'm here!' Then he would laugh and lift me up, and I'd wind my skinny arms round his neck and press my cheek to his rough one. To me he was the strongest and most handsome man in the world, and when he kept hold of me to kiss my mother, I felt utterly safe.

'Hello, Dad.' There was a constriction in my throat, and my voice sounded thin and squeezed.

'How have you been?'

'Fine. Good. I've just got a new job, in fact.'

I waited for him to congratulate me, or at least ask me what I was going to be doing, but before he could speak Saffron burst into the room the way I had been unable to do.

'Frith! You're here!' she said extravagantly. 'I've been waiting for you for *ever*! Where's George? Oh, I can't wait to show you your dress!' Without waiting for a reply, she enveloped me in a hug. 'We're going to have such fun!'

My father's expression sharpened. 'Who's George?'

'A friend,' I said stiffly, longing all at once for George to be there beside me.

'He's more than a friend, Daddy. Frith's in love!' Saffron laughed and turned to me. 'Don't pretend you're not, Frith. I've seen you together.'

Dad's brows drew together. 'What do you know about this George?'

I didn't answer. I was staring at Saffron in dismay, while my heart plummeted, bounced, crashed down again. *Frith's in love*, she had said. *Don't pretend you're not.*

How long had I been pretending? Of *course* I was in love with him. I had done exactly what I swore wouldn't do. I had let down my guard, let myself go. I had jumped into the abyss, and now look how much it was going to hurt.

'He's lovely, Daddy,' Saffron answered for me. 'He's just right for Frith. They're perfect together. He is coming, isn't he? And Roly?'

'Of course.' My lips felt stiff, and I lifted my chin at my father's glower. 'You'll meet him at the rehearsal dinner. I thought you wanted to have some family time this week?'

'I do.' Saffron clapped her hands together. 'Daddy, come out to lunch with us to celebrate!'

'Now, precious,' he said indulgently, patting her as she hung on his arm. 'You know I've meetings. You and Frith go and enjoy yourselves,' he said when she pouted. 'Buy yourselves something nice.'

That was his answer to everything: take the money and go away.

It was a long week. Saffron was even more skittish than usual, alternating between suffocating affection and tantrums. 'Is everything OK?' I asked once in a rare moment of stillness while we were getting ready to go out.

'Why wouldn't it be?' she said instantly.

'Nothing…it's just…we haven't seen much of Jax.'

'He's busy,' said Saffron. 'Anyway, we're not like you and George, all over each other the whole time.' She jumped up. 'Oh, I forgot to tell you! Dad's girlfriend has gone to Australia to shoot some show, so she won't be at the wedding after all. I'm not sorry she won't be there, but she might have thought about my seating plan! Now, show me what you're going to wear tonight.'

Saffron was appalled by my clothes. She insisted on buying me a whole new wardrobe, and she was in such a brittle mood that I let her, although there was no way I was going to be able to wear any of it in Shofrar.

Every time we went out, we had to run the gauntlet of the paparazzi, with the deafening whirr and click of the cameras and shouts to Saffron to look their way. She barely noticed the flash lights that made me squint as I stumbled after her, but I found them exhausting and I longed to be back at Whellerby.

I was glad when it was time to go to the castle Dad had taken over for the wedding. A vast, spectacularly ornate building, Castle Peart dwarfed Whellerby Hall, with none of its faintly shabby charm. Everything at the castle was glossed up and so luxurious it was suffocating. We had the spa to ourselves for a day before the others started to arrive. I'd never been much of a one for pampering but I hoped it would relax Saffron. She was so thin and tense, I was afraid that she was going to snap like a twig.

Still, the rehearsal went off without a hitch, although I was worried by the way Saffron and Jax avoided eye contact. I just had to get through tonight, I told myself, as I got ready for the rehearsal dinner. The wedding was the next day, and then it would be over.

CHAPTER TEN

BY THE time I waited with Saffron and Dad in the great hall of the castle to greet those guests lucky enough to have a coveted invitation to the rehearsal dinner, I was exhausted and nearly as twitchy as my sister.

Gradually the hall filled with famous faces. I heard from a waitress that the paparazzi were going wild at the gates. Rumours were going round about extravagant ruses to get in and scoop the photos. Hard-faced men from *Glitz*, which had bought the rights to the photos, patrolled the hall on the lookout for illicit cameras while their official photographers clicked away. I managed to dodge out of their way. I knew no one would be interested in me and, anyway, I was waiting for George and Roly.

Where were they? I tugged at the dress Saffron had made me buy. A traffic-stopping red, it was short and strappy, with a fabric that clung to every curve, and I was unsteady on vertiginous heels with jewelled straps wrapped around my ankle.

Rarely had I felt as uncomfortable or exposed. I'd been trying to make small talk, but what did I have to say to those people, swooping on each other with raucous cries, exchanging air kisses? They weren't interested in environmentally sound insulation systems or quality testing for steel reinforcing bars, and I wasn't interested in Paris fashion or the latest celebrity gossip.

I didn't belong there, any more than I belonged any-where. I seemed to have spent my whole life standing at the edge of a party, I thought. I was certain that everyone was avoiding me and a wave of loneliness and insecurity hit me with such force that I actually wobbled on my heels.

Then George walked in, and the world tilted and slid back into position with what I could have sworn was an audible click.

He stood with Roly, his eyes searching the crowded hall. For a moment I didn't move, I just drank in the sight of him. The light glinted on his hair, and I saw women's heads turn with interest, but for once I didn't notice how good look-ing he was. I didn't think about the blue eyes or the heart-clenching line of his jaw or that devastating crease in cheek. I just saw George.

George, who was looking for me. His gaze crossed mine, then caught, and his face lit up with a smile, and it felt as if a hand had reached inside my chest and were squeezing my heart so hard I could hardly breathe.

I forgot my uncomfortable dress. I hurried through the press of people towards him, but at the last minute one of those ridiculous heels caught on the edge of a flagstone and I pitched forward into George's arms.

This, this *is where you belong.* My body seemed to shout with the certainty of it.

'That's what I call a welcome!' George said, making the most of the opportunity to feel me up as he set me on my feet.

'I'm so glad to see you!' I kissed him fervently. 'And you, Roly,' I added with a smile.

'You l-look…am-azing,' Roly stuttered.

'Saffron made me wear it.' I plucked self-consciously at the clinging fabric. 'I feel half naked.'

'That's good. It's the kind of dress that makes a man determined to get you completely naked as soon as possible,' said George with grin. 'That means we're halfway there.' He turned me so that he could view me from every angle. 'How does it come off?'

I was feeling better already. 'That's something you're going to have to work out for yourself,' I said pertly.

Saffron descended with a squeal just then, dragging my father over to introduce him to them. Roly turned crimson when she kissed him, but my father was looking at my hand that was still entwined with George's. His beetly grey brows snapped together and I had to resist the urge to tug it away. George must have sensed it because his fingers tightened.

'Challoner?' Dad barked as Saffron drew Roly away. 'Not one of the banking Challoners?'

'Not any more,' said George evenly.

'What does that mean?'

'I don't work for the bank any more.'

'Well, you'd better not be sniffing around my daughter in the hope of an easy living,' my father growled. 'She's too stiff-necked to take a penny from me! If that's the way she wants it, that's fine by me. Saffron can have it instead. At least *she's* a loving daughter!'

I set my teeth. 'I don't need your money, Dad.'

'No, you don't need anything, do you? You're always so damned sure you can do it all by yourself!'

He turned away in disgust, and I bit down hard on my lip to stop the tears that clogged my throat. I was barely aware of George's arm coming round me.

'You know what?' he said. 'I think your father loves you a lot.'

'He's got a funny way of showing it!'

'I know,' he said gently, 'but I think I'm right.'

I shook my head, but I didn't want to argue. I was too glad he was there.

Every moment of that evening was recorded by the photographers from *Glitz*. Jax, it seemed, had sold the rights to the wedding photos for a ridiculous amount of money. I didn't understand it. Why did they need more money? Saffron already had more than they could possibly know what to do with.

What should have been a family ceremony had turned into a business in which all sorts of people had a vested interest, and I was dreading the next day. It didn't feel like a wedding at all. It felt like a performance. My father had spent unspeakably large sums flying in rock stars for his little girl's big day, and Saffron's dress was a stupendous creation designed to make people gasp. The house was full of people making a fortune out of the wedding, publicists and stylists and event managers. I longed for it to be over.

But none of it seemed so bad with George there.

George had worked out how to take off my dress by the time we got to bed.

The really dangerous thing, I realised, lying snuggled up next to him afterwards, was that I wanted to talk to him as much as I wanted to make love to him. I told him about shopping with Saffron and how worried I was about the lack of connection between her and Jax. He told me a funny story about Frank and the barmaid from The Whellerby Arms, and passed on a verbal report from Hugh about progress on site and made me laugh.

Only then did I realise how tense I'd been all week. I fell asleep pressed against George's warm, solid body and refused to let myself think about how much I was going to miss him.

'I can't do it,' said Saffron.

The other bridesmaids were gathered in the suite next door and I was shaking out the long beaded train while she stood in front of the cheval mirror. She looked beautiful, but unreal, like someone modelling a bride's dress.

'Sorry?' I said.

'I can't get married. I just can't.' She started shaking as I stared at her, aghast. 'But this wedding, it's cost Dad millions, and *Glitz* have bought the photos…Oh, God, Frith, what am I going to do?'

Pulling myself together, I put my arm around her shoulders. 'Well, the first thing is not to worry about *Glitz*.' I met her eyes in the mirror. 'You don't have to do anything you don't want to do, Saffron, but tell me what's happened.'

'Jax and I just don't have what you and George have. I watched you two last night. Even when he wasn't touching you, you were connected somehow. I saw the way you looked at each other, just a glance or a smile. I don't think I spoke to Jax all night,' she said bitterly.

'It's difficult when there are so many guests to talk to.' It came to something when I was making excuses for Jax.

'He shouldn't be able to keep his hands off me!'

'No,' I said. 'He shouldn't.'

'And he slept with a girl on the tour,' said Saffron abruptly. 'He said it didn't mean anything. He thinks it doesn't matter, but I think it does.'

'It matters all right,' I said.

'Will you tell Dad?' Saffron pleaded in a tiny voice. '*Please*,' she said. 'Please, Frith. I can't do it. He's going to be so disappointed in me.'

'He loves you, Saffron. Nothing's going to change that.'

'I can't do it.' Her voice started to rise, and I held up a hand.

'OK, OK, I'll do it. Don't cry. Let me think.'

I called George on his phone. He and Roly were in the spectacular star-shaped chamber where the ceremony was due to take place. 'What's going on?' he said, whispering.

'Can you come up here? I need you!'

He knocked on Saffron's door a few minutes later, Roly behind him.

I practically dragged them into the room and explained the situation. 'We have to get Saffron out of here before the publicists and everyone else get wind of what's going on.' I was already having a hard time keeping the other bridesmaids at bay.

'Absolutely,' said Roly. 'We can't have her being pestered by reporters. It's all very distressing for her.' He drew himself up. 'Let me take her to Whellerby Hall until the worst of the publicity is over and she's decided what she wants to do.'

So Saffron quickly changed out of her gown, threw a few clothes in a bag, shoved on a hat to disguise her distinctive hair and George snuck them out of the servants' entrance to Roly's car.

'They've gone,' he said when he came back. 'They followed a florist's van out the back gate.'

'OK.' I wiped my hands on my bridesmaid's dress and sucked in a breath. I was dreading this. 'Now I need to tell my father.'

George came with me to where Dad was pacing at the top of the great staircase.

'Where's Saffron?' he demanded when he saw me. 'We're over half an hour late!'

'Dad, I'm sorry, but she's decided she doesn't want to get married after all,' I said.

'*What*?' roared my father. 'Is this some kind of joke?'

I shook my head. 'She's gone.'

'But…but…' Before my horrified eyes I saw my father's face contort and, clutching at his chest, he toppled forward onto me.

* * *

I don't know what I would have done without George.

It was George who called a doctor while I panicked over my father, George who drew Jax and his best man aside so that I could break the news.

Jax, understandably, was furious. 'We had a deal!' he kept shouting. '*Glitz* have already paid us for the photos!' It seemed to me that he was far more upset about the loss of money than the fact that Saffron had left.

It was left to me to tell the guests what had happened, but it was George again who gently but firmly persuaded the wedding party to disperse. The paparazzi outside the castle went wild when they realised what had happened, and I was glad Saffron was safely away with Roly.

I went to sit with my father. The doctor said that it wasn't a heart attack as I'd feared when he crashed over me, but the stress had brought on a seizure. His face was still grey, and his eyes were closed, but he opened them as I leant over him in concern.

'Saffron's safe,' I said. 'With a friend.'

'Why did she do it? I thought she wanted this wedding,' he said, his fingers clutching querulously at his sheet. I had a sudden, sharp vision of what he would look like when he was old.

'Better to realise it's a mistake now than go through a divorce,' I said. 'You wouldn't want that for her, would you?'

'Is this all my fault?' I'd never heard him say that before.

'No.'

'I just wanted her to be happy,' he said, and he sounded so wretched with worry that I put out my hand without thinking and covered his.

'I know you do, Dad,' I said.

There was a pause, and then he turned his hand up to clutch my fingers. 'I know you don't believe me but I want you to be happy too,' he said.

My throat was so tight I couldn't speak. 'I am happy,' I managed eventually.

'With this George?'

I swallowed. 'For now,' I said.

I went back to London with him. There was no way Saffron could come back with the paparazzi camped outside the door, his girlfriend apparently wasn't bothered enough to fly back from Australia, and there was no one else. It wasn't as if Dad would have been alone—he had servants and a PA and any number of employees in and out whole time—but he'd looked so old and wretched, I couldn't bring myself to leave him on his own.

Without Saffron, my father and I had little choice but to talk to each other. Our conversations were often spiky and we disagreed about almost everything, but at least they were never boring. Dad hated the fact that I refused to accept any money from him.

'Stop trying to buy me!' I said in exasperation at last. 'You've always done that!'

'I just wanted you to need me,' he said. He must have been feeling low, or he would never have said anything that unguarded.

'I did need you, Dad,' I said after a moment. 'But I needed a father, not a bank account.' I hesitated. 'I still do.'

No more was said but when I went to say goodbye, he opened his arms hesitantly. I bit my lip, then went into them, and felt them close around me as they had done when I was a little girl. He didn't say anything, but he held me very tightly, and my chest was tight when I stepped away.

'You'll let me know how you get on in Shofrar?' he said gruffly, and I nodded. Suddenly it didn't matter that he could see that I was close to the tears that always made me feel so weak.

'I'll keep in touch,' I promised, and he pressed his lips, exactly the way I did when I was struggling not to cry.

'I'd like to hear from you,' he said after a moment. 'Thank you, Frith.'

I wouldn't take any money, but I let him send me back to Whellerby in luxury. His chauffeur took me all the way to the cottage door.

The last few days I had wanted to spend with George had gone. I had only two days for a last visit to site, to put Audrey up on blocks and to say my goodbyes.

Perhaps it was all for the best, I told myself. Driving back into Whellerby had felt dangerously like going home. George had cooked a welcome home/farewell dinner and Saffron and Roly were there. To my surprise, Saffron had taken to country life in a big way. I couldn't quite work out her relationship with Roly but she seemed happy, and George was even teaching her to ride.

Saffron couldn't understand why I was going. 'Do you know how lucky you are to have George? He's a nice man and he loves you, and you love him.'

'I need more than love, Saffron,' I told her. 'There's nothing for me to do in Whellerby now. George understands that.'

He said he did, anyway. Of course I had imagined staying, but I wasn't interested in pottering around the house. I had to work. It had been a long hard slog to get qualified. I was where I had planned to be, and the next step was clear.

'And you, you need to be here,' I said to George that last night. 'Running the estate, working with horses the way you planned. That's what you've always wanted. You need a family, George. You should find a girl who wants those things too.'

'What if I don't want a girl like that?' said George. 'What

if I want *you*?' He took my hands. 'I love you, Frith. You know that, don't you?'

The blue eyes held an expression I had never seen before, and my blood tingled as I stared into them, my fingers curled tightly around his. Saffron had said that he loved me, and at some level I think I had known that it was true, but this was the first time that George had said it out loud. The first time I had really let myself believe it.

It was amazing. Incredibly, extraordinarily, wonderfully amazing. George loved me. George, who was so warm and so funny and so true. He was a good man, an intelligent man, and wiser than I had ever given him credit for. He was knee-wobblingly gorgeous. And he loved *me*. Small wonder my heart was swelling and singing!

He *loved* me.

'And I love you,' I said. 'Oh, George, I do, I *do*!'

'Then stay.'

'I can't,' I said and my voice cracked.

I didn't dare. He might love me now, but how could he love me for ever? He needed to love someone kind and sweet and nice who would belong in his world. How could he truly love a prickly misfit like me?

'I do love you, George,' I tried to explain. 'There's a huge bit of me that longs to say "yes, I'll stay" and find myself some kind of job, but what would I do? You know what I'm like. I'd end up snappy and resentful, and take it out on you. I'd hate it if that happened and you stopped loving me.'

'I won't stop loving you,' said George, his clasp warm and steady. 'You have to trust me.'

'I...can't,' I said brokenly. I wanted to—oh, how I wanted to!—but I couldn't shake the memory of my mother, who had trusted Dad to love her for ever too. I couldn't bear to let myself need George and then to lose him. I couldn't bear to spend the rest of my life missing him. It was better to say goodbye while we were still friends.

'I'm sorry, George,' I whispered. 'I just can't.'

George drove me to the airport near Leeds. I was flying to London and then straight out to Shofrar. My bags were packed. I said goodbye to Roly and Saffron, and gave Audrey a last pat. I had nothing more to stay for.

We were silent on the drive. I wanted to find the words to tell George how much I'd loved him, how important his friendship had been to me, how much I was going to miss him. But I couldn't speak. My throat was too tight, my heart too full. I was horribly afraid that if I opened my mouth, it would be to ask him to turn around and take me home.

'Don't come in,' I said when we got to the airport. 'It's going to be hard enough saying goodbye as it is.'

'All right.' George lifted my case out of the back of the car and set it on a trolley. Straightened, he looked at me and his jaw tightened. 'So, this is goodbye?'

'Yes,' I said, and my voice broke as I stepped forward and held onto him tightly, squeezing my eyes shut against the treacherous tears as his arms came round me for a last time. 'I'll never forget you,' I said. 'I do love you, I do, it's just—'

He stopped me, laying a finger across my lips. 'I know,' he said, 'the plan.'

We kissed, a last desperate kiss, and then I pulled away before I changed my mind. 'Goodbye, George,' I managed, reaching blindly for the trolley, and then I walked away from him.

I walked away from the best chance of happiness I ever had because I was afraid of how much I loved him and how deeply he made me feel. I walked away from a wonderful man who loved me and who made me laugh, away from the hope of a family, away from the only place I felt as if I belonged. I'd spent years fearing to let go in case some-one hurt me, but in the end, when I let go anyway, I broke my own heart.

I turned my back and I didn't look back, so that George couldn't see the tears I had kept bottled up inside me for so long pouring uncontrollably down my cheeks.

It was all for the best. I told myself that a lot. And I *was* glad I was in Shofrar. I loved my job. It was a huge site, and I got a buzz out of being involved in such a big, complex project. I loved the harsh light and the hammering sun and the wail of the muezzin sent shivers down my spine.

I'd never been anywhere remotely like Shofrar before. It was a small but prosperous state with a Westernised approach that made it easier for me as a woman. I could drive and live alone. There was a compound with rows of prefabricated houses, and I was allotted one of those. Social life was fairly restricted. There was a club in the compound, and at weekends we could go down to the sea and drink beers at the beach club, but that was it.

I wasn't the only female engineer there but we were massively outnumbered by the men, and I had no shortage of offers to play as well as work together. I stuck to group outings though. The thought of anyone but George touching me made me feel physically sick. I missed him with a horrible dragging ache.

I missed his touch, terribly, but I missed talking to him more. I missed the gleam in his eyes when he was teasing me, the tantalising curl of his mouth, his smile as he drew me towards him. I missed coming home at the end of the day and finding him there with his feet on my table, drinking my beer. I missed arguing with him, laughing with him. I missed my friend. I missed my lover.

My ringtone was a sensibly discreet buzz. I hated it.

But I had my career, I reminded myself feverishly. I couldn't have both. The number of times I sat down and looked at the phone, thinking about ringing George and hearing his voice. The times my fingers hovered over the keyboard when I was at my email. Whenever something happened, my first thought was how I would tell George about it.

I didn't get in touch. What would have been the point? I'd made my decision. Besides—I tortured myself with this thought a lot—George had probably met someone else by now. Someone pretty who loved the country and rode horses and laughed at all his jokes. Someone who wouldn't roll their eyes when he drank their beer or argue with him or insist on going to work overseas. He had said he loved me, but how long would he miss me?

It was a long day on site. The heat was crushing, and the sand and dust were gritty on my skin. My head throbbed under the hard hat, not helped by the roar of the great earth movers. Everything had gone wrong that day, and by the time I got back to my characterless quarters I wanted nothing more than to take a long, cold shower and fall onto my bed. Still, I found myself reluctant to go back. The house felt empty and every time I opened the door and faced the silence broken only by the rattle of the air conditioner my loneliness increased.

There was a car parked outside the house. It was dark and official-looking and I looked at it puzzled as I drew up bumper to bumper. Leaving my hard hat in my pickup truck, I got out and glanced curiously at the driver as I closed my door, only to freeze. He had fair hair like George, shoulders set just like George's, and the glimpse was like a punch to my heart.

Then he opened his own door and got out, and the tarmac beneath my feet tilted, making my head reel. It couldn't be George.

But it was. Incredibly, he looked nervous, but it was George. He took off his sunglasses and looked straight at me, and my heart, which had stopped with that first blow of recognition, stuttered back to life.

'George,' I croaked. 'George.'

'Hello, Frith.'

I didn't think. I just walked into his arms. 'George.' It was all I could say as he folded me tightly to him.

We didn't kiss at first. We just clung together, and I breathed in the wonderful smell of him. I still couldn't really believe that he was real, that he was there. 'George. I thought I'd never see you again.'

'I've missed you,' he murmured against my hair. 'God, I've missed you.'

I lifted my face from his throat at last. 'What are you doing here? No wait,' I said when he began to answer. 'Let's go inside. It's too hot out here.'

I let him into the blissful cool of the house. My legs were shaking, and I leant back against the door as I closed it. 'What *are* you doing here?'

George didn't answer immediately. He was looking around the room, and I could see how bare it must look to his eyes. I hadn't had the heart to personalise it. 'How's the job?' he asked.

'Good,' I said. 'I'm enjoying it.' It was true. 'It's what I want to do, George.'

'I know that.'

The air conditioning rattled into the silence.

'How are things at Whellerby?' I asked at last. 'Is everything all right?'

'Fine,' said George. 'Saffron and Roly are getting mar-

ried next summer. They want me to be best man and you
to be bridesmaid.'

'I'm not sure I can cope with another of Saffron's weddings!'

'She promises this one is going to be small, in Whellerby
church. Roly's ecstatic, as you can imagine.'

'And Saffron?' I asked dubiously.

'She's happy too. You wouldn't think it, but they're well
suited.'

'Roly will adore her, and she'll adore being adored.'

'They're very sweet together,' said George. 'I'm pleased
for them both, of course, but I miss you. There's only so
much sweetness I can take.'

He came over to take my hands and draw me away from
the door, his clasp warm and firm. 'I can't tell you how
much I've missed you, Frith.'

'I've missed you too,' I told him, but my heart was sinking. He was going to ask me to go back, and I was going to
have to say no. I couldn't give up the job now. I was learn-
ing so much.

'I'm not going to ask you to come back,' said George,
not for the first time reading my mind.

'Oh. Oh, right.' I know, I'm perverse, but my first re-
action was bitter disappointment. I struggled to sound as
if I didn't care. 'So what are you doing here?' I asked for
the third time.

'I've come for an interview.'

It was the last thing I'd expected him to say. 'An *interview*?'

'For a job,' he said helpfully.

'But…the estate…the stables…'

'The stables will always be there, and Saffron's looking
after Mabel. The family have "forgiven" me, apparently,
and they offered me the money to set up a remedial centre,

but I don't want to take it. I want to do it by myself, and I can earn good money if I get this job. And I probably *will* get the job,' George said. 'I might not take their money, but I'm cashing in my connections. Harry set this up for me.'

'What job?' I said, puzzled. I couldn't imagine what George could do out in Shofrar.

'I'd forgotten, but the Sultan of Shofrar was in the same class as Harry at school. They met up in London recently at some banking affair, and the Sultan told Harry that he wanted to set up a stud. Shofrari Arab horses used to be famous, and he's keen to build up their reputation again. It turns out that he's looking for an advisor, and Harry mentioned me…I got the impression the job's mine if I want it.'

I couldn't take it in. 'But you want a life in the country,' I stammered.

'Not without you,' said George. 'I tried, Frith, I really did. I went through all the stages. I was wretched after you left, then furious with you for going. Then I told myself that I had to accept it and get on with my life. I kept psyching myself up to meet someone else, but then I realised that I didn't want anyone else. I only want you.'

'But I'm so…so…' My fingers twined around George's of their own accord.

'You're not easy, I'll grant you,' he said. 'You're prickly and practical and far, far too attached to your plans, but it was you I wanted to talk to when I got in at the end of the day. I wanted you to make me laugh. I wanted that feeling of rightness I got when I held you.

'You said we were different,' he went on when I could only gaze dumbly at him, 'and we are, but we fit together anyway, and I miss that and I want it again, and if the only way I can be with you is to come out and be where your job is, that's what I'll do.'

I swallowed the constriction in my throat. 'I can't believe you'd do that for me.'

'I'll do it for *us*, if you want it.'

'Oh, George, yes, I want it.' My voice broke as I reached for him. 'I've been so unhappy without you.'

'But there's a condition,' said George, and I pulled back a little.

'Condition?'

'You have to marry me,' he said. 'I know how you feel about marriage, sweetheart,' he said, gathering me back against him. 'I know you're afraid, and that trusting is hard for you, but if you love me, you're going to have to prove it. I think you don't believe anyone could really love you, but I do. Believing me is a risk for you, I know, but you're going to have to take it.

'There are no guarantees, Frith,' he said. 'I can't promise that everything will always go according to plan, but we can promise to hold together and trust each other. We'll both need to do some giving and some taking. Maybe you'll get a job somewhere else one day. Maybe we'll decide to spend some time near Whellerby again. Happiness isn't about place, it's about being together. We don't know what's going to happen, but we can agree that whatever we face, we face it together, that if there are decisions to be made, we make them together.'

His blue eyes searched my face. 'That means giving up your independence, yes. If we get married, we'll be a shared enterprise from now on and it won't always be easy. It's up to you to decide if it's worth it, if you love me enough to take the risk. If you don't, I'll go back to Whellerby and the Sultan can find another advisor for his stud.'

I looked at George, loving every line of him. I thought about my mother, and how lonely she had been without Dad. It had been easy for me to blame him, but I didn't know what had happened. Maybe they had both missed chances to make the marriage work. At least they had tried.

Was *I* brave enough to try?

Then I thought about waking up with George every morning, about going home to him every evening. I thought about the way he drove me mad and made me laugh and understood me the way nobody else had ever done. George accepted me for what I was and all he asked in return was that I believed in him. That didn't seem so much to ask.

I couldn't spend my life being afraid of feeling, I realised. I had a chance to spend it with a man who made my heart sing. Was I really going to turn my back on that again? The abyss still yawned before me, but this time I knew exactly what I had to do.

'So it's marriage or nothing?' I peeped a glance at him under my lashes.

'That's the deal,' said George firmly.

'Then I'll take the risk if you will.'

A slow smile started in the blue eyes and lit up his whole face, and only then did I realise that he really hadn't been sure how I would answer. George lifted me up and swung me round with a shout of triumph. 'We'll take it together,' he said, and kissed me.

It was much later when I stirred against him. I traced a pattern on his chest with a fingertip.

'There's just one thing that bothers me about this marriage idea.'

George opened one eye. 'Only one? Well, that's a step forward.'

'Funny you should mention steps,' I said, propping myself up on one elbow so that I could look down into his face. 'I would really feel happier if we could have *some* sort of plan.'

'Ah, I see where you're going,' said George indulgently. 'You think we should set ourselves some SMART goals?'

'We can be flexible about how we get there, but I like to know where I'm going.'

'All right, let me see…' He took my hair and tucked it behind my ears. 'Our goal is to build a strong and lasting marriage. Is that specific enough for you?'

'Yes, but is it measurable?'

'We'll know if it's strong,' said George, 'as long as we're both prepared to compromise, so it's definitely attainable, if we take it one day at a time.'

I had a momentary doubt. 'But is it realistic?'

'It'll mean talking and laughing and loving. What's more realistic than that?'

'It *might* work,' I acknowledged. My fingertip crept lower, circling, circling. 'We can't make our goal time-bound, though, can we?'

George pretended to give it some thought. 'I don't know about that. How does forever sound to you?' he said, and I smiled as I leant over to kiss him.

'It sounds perfect.'

* * * * *

Mills & Boon® Hardback

November 2012

ROMANCE

A Night of No Return	Sarah Morgan
A Tempestuous Temptation	Cathy Williams
Back in the Headlines	Sharon Kendrick
A Taste of the Untamed	Susan Stephens
Exquisite Revenge	Abby Green
Beneath the Veil of Paradise	Kate Hewitt
Surrendering All But Her Heart	Melanie Milburne
Innocent of His Claim	Janette Kenny
The Price of Fame	Anne Oliver
One Night, So Pregnant!	Heidi Rice
The Count's Christmas Baby	Rebecca Winters
His Larkville Cinderella	Melissa McClone
The Nanny Who Saved Christmas	Michelle Douglas
Snowed in at the Ranch	Cara Colter
Hitched!	Jessica Hart
Once A Rebel...	Nikki Logan
A Doctor, A Fling & A Wedding Ring	Fiona McArthur
Her Christmas Eve Diamond	Scarlet Wilson

MEDICAL

Maybe This Christmas...?	Alison Roberts
Dr Chandler's Sleeping Beauty	Melanie Milburne
Newborn Baby For Christmas	Fiona Lowe
The War Hero's Locked-Away Heart	Louisa George

Mills & Boon® Large Print

November 2012

ROMANCE

The Secrets She Carried — Lynne Graham
To Love, Honour and Betray — Jennie Lucas
Heart of a Desert Warrior — Lucy Monroe
Unnoticed and Untouched — Lynn Raye Harris
Argentinian in the Outback — Margaret Way
The Sheikh's Jewel — Melissa James
The Rebel Rancher — Donna Alward
Always the Best Man — Fiona Harper
A Royal World Apart — Maisey Yates
Distracted by her Virtue — Maggie Cox
The Count's Prize — Christina Hollis

HISTORICAL

An Escapade and an Engagement — Annie Burrows
The Laird's Forbidden Lady — Ann Lethbridge
His Makeshift Wife — Anne Ashley
The Captain and the Wallflower — Lyn Stone
Tempted by the Highland Warrior — Michelle Willingham

MEDICAL

Sydney Harbour Hospital: Lexi's Secret — Melanie Milburne
West Wing to Maternity Wing! — Scarlet Wilson
Diamond Ring for the Ice Queen — Lucy Clark
No.1 Dad in Texas — Dianne Drake
The Dangers of Dating Your Boss — Sue MacKay
The Doctor, His Daughter and Me — Leonie Knight

Mills & Boon® Hardback
December 2012

ROMANCE

A Ring to Secure His Heir	Lynne Graham
What His Money Can't Hide	Maggie Cox
Woman in a Sheikh's World	Sarah Morgan
At Dante's Service	Chantelle Shaw
At His Majesty's Request	Maisey Yates
Breaking the Greek's Rules	Anne McAllister
The Ruthless Caleb Wilde	Sandra Marton
The Price of Success	Maya Blake
The Man From her Wayward Past	Susan Stephens
Blame it on the Bikini	Natalie Anderson
The English Lord's Secret Son	Margaret Way
The Secret That Changed Everything	Lucy Gordon
Baby Under the Christmas Tree	Teresa Carpenter
The Cattleman's Special Delivery	Barbara Hannay
Secrets of the Rich & Famous	Charlotte Phillips
Her Man In Manhattan	Trish Wylie
His Bride in Paradise	Joanna Neil
Christmas Where She Belongs	Meredith Webber

MEDICAL

From Christmas to Eternity	Caroline Anderson
Her Little Spanish Secret	Laura Iding
Christmas with Dr Delicious	Sue MacKay
One Night That Changed Everything	Tina Beckett

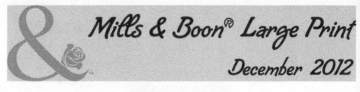

Mills & Boon® Large Print

December 2012

ROMANCE

HISTORICAL

MEDICAL